1/23 £1

BEAST

Paul Kingsnorth's debut novel, *The Wake* won the 2014 Gordon Burn Prize, was longlisted for the Man Booker Prize, the Folio Prize and the Desmond Elliot Prize, and was shortlisted for the Goldsmith's Prize. He is also the author of two non-fiction books, *One No, Many Yeses* and *Real England*, and a poetry collection, *Kidland*. He is co-founder of the Dark Mountain Project, a global network of writers, artists and thinkers in search of new stories for a world on the brink.

Further praise for *Beast*:

'Eerily arresting . . . the book brings to mind such films as Robin Hardy's *The Wicker Man* and Michael Reeves's *Witchfinder General* . . . There is much potent writing, calm wisdom and quiet understanding in this book.' *Literary Review*

'This is a powerful, claustrophobic novel, rendered with a minimum of the usual literary props, coaxing us into a single, damaged mind that disarmingly illustrates the universal condition.' Adam Thorpe, *Times Literary Supplement*

'Prose a⸺ ⸺th's

gaze is so intense it forces a similar intensity from the reader. The smallest shift of the light puts us on edge, on our mettle. Will something terrible happen? The moor, an empty church, an empty lane with something glimpsed swiftly crossing it – all are so menacing because they are so minutely themselves.'
M. John Harrison, *Guardian* 'Book of the Day'

'Although written in our tongue, the language is still relentless, even brutal . . . [a] strange, elusive book.' *Spectator*

'With its ruggedly handsome descriptions of nature and portentous spiritual self-reflection . . . the spell is never broken.' *Telegraph*

'A potent, chilling but intoxicating fable, one that builds in unbearable intensity and beguiles with unflinching prose.' *Herald*

---

by the same author

fiction
THE WAKE

non-fiction
ONE NO, MANY YESES
REAL ENGLAND
UNCIVILISATION (with Dougald Hine)

poetry
KIDLAND AND OTHER POEMS

PAUL KINGSNORTH

BEAST

FABER & FABER

First published in 2016
by Faber & Faber Limited
Bloomsbury House
74–77 Great Russell Street
London WC1B 3DA
This paperback edition first published in 2017

Typeset by Faber & Faber Limited
Printed in the UK by CPI Group (UK) Ltd, Croydon, CR0 4YY

A CIP record for this book
is available from the British Library

ISBN 978–0–571–32208–4

FSC
www.fsc.org
MIX
Paper from
responsible sources
FSC® C020471

2 4 6 8 10 9 7 5 3 1

It could be that God has not absconded but spread, as our vision and understanding of the universe have spread, to a fabric of spirit and sense so grand and subtle, so powerful in a new way, that we can only feel blindly at its hem.

Annie Dillard

And where we had thought to find an abomination, we shall find a god; where we had thought to slay another, we shall slay ourselves; where we had thought to travel outward, we shall come to the centre of our own existence; where we had thought to be alone, we shall be with all the world.

Joseph Campbell

I stood in the river up to my knees and the river was cold. The water filled my boots and made its way up through the fabric of my trousers towards my groin. Soon I couldn't feel my feet, and soon after that I couldn't feel my legs. The river sang and kept singing. I wanted to clamber out, but I stood still. Pain rose and tried to encircle me, but I stood in the winter torrent and watched the pain and after a while it fell back again, back down into the singing water.

Water came down from the clouds and sank through the black peat and passed over the granite and then went down through its channel to the sea. The water that ran over my legs and feet would never be seen here again but the river never changed. I climbed into the river in the early morning and I stood there until the sun was highest in the sky. I let the water take my body away from me so that I could see what was beyond my body. I let the river numb me and I understood that I had always been numb. The sky opened a crack, but only a crack. There was still something beyond that I could not touch.

Water, thorns, rain, black soil. All of the pain is an incident, a detail soon forgotten. From the east I came, from the dead fens, because of everything that grew there, because of what was lodged in the dark waters. I walked the streets, I sat on the couches, I passed through the sliding doors, I talked but never listened, I sold but never gave away. Everywhere there were voices and I added my voice to them and we spoke out together and said nothing at all. I became entwined in wanting, and it took me away from the stillness that is everything. I say it here daily now like a prayer, like an offering: it is everything, it is everything, and sometimes I glimpse it and then I am every storm wind that has ever run itself clean across the black of the sea.

From the east I came, to this high place, to be broken, to be torn apart, beaten, cut into pieces. I came here to measure myself against the great emptiness. I came here to touch the void, to leap naked into it with the shards of what I was falling around me, to have the void clean me of the smallness that I swam in. To come out white and empty with a small, sharp piece of that emptiness in me always, because it is all that can ever save me. To be open, to be in fear, to be aching with nothingness, to be lonely as the cold subsoil in winter, lonely as the last whale in the ocean, singing in bewilderment and no other to answer for all of time. This darkness.

This is the only life.

I haven't been sleeping well. I see things when I close my eyes. Old things climb out through my mouth and set themselves free in the air. On the high moor there are patterns and in my small mind there are patterns, and my breath fogs on the windows here and when I leave a footprint in the yard it stays for weeks. There are movements at night and I don't understand them. Strange things rise up when the cars full of tourists go home and the farm lights burn yellow on the far slopes. All the centuries drop away, and I am in the presence of something that does not know time.

Five seasons I've been here now. Five seasons, but I've never seen a storm like this. An hour or two back, I stood by the door and watched it rise over the shoulder of the moor. Winter here is one long storm, dark and roiling, the wind tearing at you, pulling you down. But this one is harder than usual, louder, stronger. It roars up the fields like a beast chasing the smell of blood. The rain is horizontal, it blows in from the west as if it has been arrowed in from the Atlantic. It forces itself through every crack, through every gap and space. It seeps through the walls, around the doors, around the windows, it runs down from the roof where the iron meets the stone, it comes through the openings where the plastic flails in the wind. It has been roaring now for an hour maybe, not much longer, but everything is getting wet. I've pushed towels and flannels and rags into every weeping cut and wound but still it comes.

I think that something is coming. I don't know what. I wonder if it will thunder, if there will be lightning. Lightning is drawn to iron. There is iron on the roof, but there is iron too in the deep rocks of the moor. I am living on and under iron, there is metal everywhere, metal and flesh and wet, black trees. I look out of the window and I see sheets of water flowing across the yard, through the gate, down onto the track. The sky is a solid darkness. Last time there was a big storm, the track from this place, which leads along the combe about a mile down to the road, became so pitted and full of great gashes that I could barely even walk on it. It was as if something had attacked it. The wind here will throw you to the ground if it catches you, will tear the slates off the roof and make them fly. Rain like this will make the streams rise so fast that they foam brown and white and roar down the combes into the valleys where the people are. And here are the stone walls and stone floors turning darker with the water, as the rain comes through the roof, and here is the stove hissing as the rain drips upon it. I am surrounded.

Five seasons. Thirteen months. Thirteen months and eight days. I wonder what they are thinking now. I wonder what they think of me. All of the weight I threw down, my retreat from the encircling, from the furious thoughts and opinions, the views and the positions soldered together with impatience and anger, enfolding the world in underwater cables and radio waves, singing in the air, darting from brain to brain, jumping from raindrop to thundercloud, glueing the world up, roaring like a storm wave. All of the energy, depleting itself in slow motion across the frozen void, running itself out for all time with nothing done, nothing even touched, everything swerved around. The sloughing entropy and nothing come from it, the wasted cells, the long dance that ends in silence. All of the fingers, the hands outstretched towards me, set to shape me.

To shape me, or to hold me?

I worry that the roof won't hold out. When I walked here shoeless over the moor from the east, with no light in the sky, I found the old farmyard dark and empty, the house and the barn echoing and broken, wet and unheld. All that passed for a roof then was a couple of twisted sheets of corrugated iron, bent back by the force of years. The rest was woodwormed rafters opening onto the blackness inside. But there was still a stove in this wet, desolate room, with its stone flag floors and its years of accumulated rot and vegetation, and the stove looked like it could be made to work, though it was covered in birdshit and rust. I had not known what I was looking for when I came looking. This old place, clinging to the moorside in the thick night, felt like an invitation.

I worked hard to shape it and make it mine. I scraped the birdshit off the stove, cleaned the windows, filled the gaps in the glass with anything I could find, scrubbed the floor clean, repaired the door lock which I had broken getting in, patched up the chimney. Then I climbed gingerly up to the roof and I nailed the bent iron back onto the soft beams as best I could. In the roofless barn across the cobbled yard I found a pile of stiff, crusted fertiliser bags beneath a cake of rotten straw. I slit them open and laid them and a worn tarpaulin over the gaps, and tied them all down with blue nylon rope. I was proud of my work, back then. This was to be my home, it was to be the place where I would sit in the silence and wait for the presence. But it is not enough tonight. The gaps between the sheets are starting to leak. Fertiliser bags can't hold up against this. The iron is rising and falling, clanging like a hammer on the black beams. Things are tearing. It sounds like some of the nails are coming loose. I'm sitting here by the stove, not looking up, willing the water not to land on the back of my neck.

Perhaps it will end soon.

I haven't been sleeping well. I think I said that. Just recently, I haven't been sleeping well. I don't know why. I've been having strange dreams. Distant lights out in the sea, fleets of swans flying, trees under water, old trees. Last night I dreamed that I was out collecting firewood on the ridge when I disturbed a hare under an ash tree. It was sandy brown, it had a white belly and black eartips, it was long-boned and sharp as the winter and there was something about its eyes that didn't fit. They didn't look like animal eyes, they seemed human, and this hare with its strange eyes it just stood there, it stood and looked into me as if it were about to speak, as if it had something to tell me, to promise, to warn me away from.

I'm used to this now. By day I walk the thin paths through the heather, I pace the farmyard, I sit cross-legged in this room for hours, I stand in thickets of thorn listening for the music on the wind. By night I dream. I wonder if home is calling me, if the flatlands want me back, or if this winter moor is just getting to me. Thirteen months is a long time to spend with only the wind to speak to. There are things out there at night that you don't want to be in the company of. Stalking through the gully, muttering along the stone row, shifting and stammering in the woods. Perhaps I have been in this dreaming too long. Perhaps I am losing my mind.

I do hope so.

The walls are soaking now, the stone is weeping, the stain is spreading across the floor. There is a creeping blackness moving towards me. There is rain dripping on the stovetop, every drip hissing angrily as it lands. This storm, this storm. It's ruining everything.

But the stove is still burning hard. A few drops of rain mean nothing to it. Often I have sat here staring through the cracked glass, watching the flames, unmoving. Daily I have sat cross-legged on the cold floor, silent, watching the unremarkable become transfigured. Stare at anything for long enough and it becomes fearful. To burn things, to burn so many things just to keep your body warm, to set this inferno raging across the world so that you can be warm and move fast, to churn the gases about, to shift the particles in the air, to slice wood with metal, to tear into the ground, to blacken the soil, to make so much heat. If I could, if I was strong enough, I would not have fire here. If I was strong enough I would never eat, I would never speak, I would never think or move, I would only sit. I would sit for two hundred years in the light and then I would know.

There is steam rising from the tin kettle now, the iron frying pan is on the stovetop and a triangle of half-frozen butter is starting to pool in it, which means that soon I can put the egg in. It's Sunday, and every Sunday I allow myself an egg. Otherwise I live on bread, potatoes, beans, water and black tea. I allow myself one bar of chocolate a month, though sometimes I worry about that. St Anthony got by in the desert on salt, bread and water. But I have earned my indulgence, and I will have it, storm or no storm. I am hungry. I am so hungry.

I wonder if I should go back. Go back east, take them what I have found here. But what would they do with it? They would have nothing to say and I would not know how to tell them. They would draw round me in a ring, baring their teeth like apes on the savannah. Everything is prey to them, everything is clay for their hands to mould, they want to eat everything, chew it all up and then excuse themselves. Back there I was an item, an object, a collection of gears, a library of facts compiled by others, a spark plug in a universal engine, an opinion machine, I was made of plastic and bamboo canes and black bin bags, I walked like I was human and alive but I was neither. I could know anything in an instant and I knew nothing at all.

No. I need to be in the places where the light comes through, where people are thin on the ground, where the old spirits still mutter in the hedges and the stone rows. But how long do I stay, and when do I know? When do I go back? Do I ever go back, and if I don't, what does that make me? What does that make this?

They grow fast. Everyone says that. You turn around one day and they're gone.

But there was no staying. I know that. There was no staying and there is no returning, not until it is done. I will know when it is done. There will be some kind of sign, some kind of feeling. Things will become clear. And when I go back, when I tell them, when I show them, they will forgive me. The things I have seen. Every saint walked away. Every holy man, every prophet, they all walked away. That's the bit they don't tell you. They never tell you about what was left behind, about who was left behind, about what had to be broken. That part of the story is always swept under, but it's the most important part of all. It's the clean break that begins everything.

I liberated them, too. I gave them their freedom. One day, they will thank me.

There it goes! There goes the tarp. It looks like one end of it is still tied down, but the rest is flapping like some giant prehistoric bird up there, lashing against the roof, and the iron sheets are even looser. There's a bloody great gap up there now, opening and closing with the wind and the rain is crashing down, sheeting in. I can't stand the rain anymore, I can't stand it, I can't. I've had it with the storm, with all the storms, with all the roaring up there, with all the noise, with everything coming down on me.

I have to do something. I will do something, I will do it if this storm doesn't slow down. I'll give it five minutes, I'll wait another five minutes, just to see if it dies back or the rain slows. I don't want to go up there. But if I wait too long the whole thing is going to come off, and then I'm right back where I started.

Perhaps it will never die back. Why should it? Why should it make this thing easy? I wanted it to be hard. It was why I came, why I was sent here. A day comes, a time is presented to each one of us, once only in our lives, and we know when it has arrived, whether we acknowledge it to ourselves or not. Something settles into us from the sky on that day or rises into us from the ground, a great stillness, a huge colour, a bottomless well of nothing and everything, a balancing, extended moment in which there is no longing at all, no past and no future, nothing that will be or has ever been. Everything in the world has been leading up to this moment but you will never have any hope of grasping it, of following its lead, if you stay here walking these paving stones and slouching in these office cubicles and buying cans in these corner shops and standing in line in these supermarkets and waiting at these bus stops in the rain.

What is this? Is it a tiny piece of the great mystery? Is this what some people call God? Does it turn out that God is not a spirit, a lord, a king, an expression of the human ego, an instructor, a giver of rewards and punishments, a fixer, a maker of rules? Does it turn out that God is not like you and me and never has been, does it turn out that God is an emptiness, a space into which life is poured and from which life re-emerges, fecund and scrabbling in the void? And does it turn out that this thing, this mystery, this void, this truth, this God – that this can only be seen when everything else, including our minds, especially our minds, has dropped or been sheared away?

You don't know. You don't know anything at all, only that you have been shown this, though you never expected to be. What will you do with it?

You know then that you have to go. There is no question of choice. You have to leave it all, find yourself a silent place, a wild place, away from the paving stones and street lamps and away from all of the people, even the ones who love you, especially them. They are the dangerous ones. Then you must sit, empty yourself, open yourself and wait for it to find you again. This is the search, it is what they have always said, all over the world, all of the seekers. These are the rules.

Once, everybody knew this, and they respected it. The hermits and the saints would arm themselves for battle and they would head out into the wild to meet the foe, and anything of themselves that they needed to strip away, they would do it to ensure victory. No-one believes that stuff anymore. They're all filling their pockets and their mouths, they're all naming the parts, they're all frantic with their unhappiness and their opinions, there is nothing you can tell them. They won't let you leave, now. And if you leave, they won't let you come back.

I never asked for any of this, so I cannot be held responsible. It is not my fault, I just followed it. I knew there would be damage. I remember what she said when she realised that this time, so late, I was finally going through with it. Are you looking for God or looking for yourself? she said. Can you even tell the difference anymore? She was clever like that. It's easy to be clever when you've always had everything, easy to be clever when it's all been laid out for you. Nothing was ever laid out for me, nobody ever showed me anything and I told her that. Six years, she said, it's been six years, and you leave now, at the worst time there could be, and for nothing. It's not for nothing, I said, I have tried to tell you. You are a child, she said, you always have been, and now I have two children. Yes, I said, I am a child, I can still see the world afresh, look at it, look! My whole life I have been sitting in silence, I have been sitting in the corner for thirty years and not speaking, now something has been shown to me, now it has all fallen away and look at me here, at last I am standing up, at last I have the guts to walk away, to walk towards what I could be. Would you stop me from being what I could be?

You do know, she said, that it is not all about you anymore? You do know that? What about her? She is

- 14 -

barely born, she's too young to know anything, she gets no kind of say, she doesn't even get a memory. Just to walk out on her. Is this the kind of man you are?

What kind of man am I? I wonder what I think about that now that I have spent a year here, watching the layers peel off, stripping myself back. You peel and peel and peel but there is always another one underneath. Does the work ever end, is there a centre, and if so what do you find down there? Some promise, some jewel, some answer? When I came, I thought that if I could spend enough years away from all of it and all of them, then the thing that was in me, the colour that had descended, the song that was singing, the thing that I could still become might emerge like a butterfly in summer, testing its dusty wings and dreaming of the sun.

That was what I thought then. I wonder what I think now. I used to know everything when I was young. Now that I'm older, I don't know anything at all. Now the mystery is the thing. There are sadhus in the temples and mendicants in the mountains, all of them struggling through in search of the mystery, in search of the white light in the grey. There are fires burning on distant hills, men standing on the prows of small boats roaring across the Java Sea, tiny people in giant canopy forests hacking through to unseen clearings while the monkeys hoot around them. We built a world of altars because we could never put the mystery into words. We tried to make the mystery human, we tried to lock it into shape, we made sacrifices to it, we sang its poetry and then we left the buildings empty and walked away. We don't talk about the mystery anymore, not where I come from, but nothing has changed in the world except us.

Come to a place like this, though, and you can still hear it sing. I can tell you that from experience. Come to a place like this, far from the estates and the ring roads and the car parks and the black fields of beet and the screen-dumb people pacing out the slow suicide of the West around the pedestrianised precincts. Come to a place like this, shut your mouth and your mind and walk on the moor, walk in the wind and the sun, and you will understand soon enough that this world is a great animal, alive and breathing, that we walk through it, we breathe with it, we are its breath, that when we stand on a mountain overcome by the sunset and all that it brings, or fall to our knees in front of an altar in the presence of something greater than ourselves, then we are sensing the animal shift and turn beneath our feet. Then it is calling us home.

Or perhaps it is hungry.

St Cuthbert was called to be a hermit on Lindisfarne. This was more than a thousand years ago. There were only small wooden huts there then, and the wind and the wild sea and everything that lived in the wild sea. Cuthbert went out there to the monastery, but the monastery was not far enough and he was called out further. He rowed to an empty island, where he ate onions and the eggs of seabirds and stood in the sea and prayed while sea otters played around his ankles. He lived there alone for years, but then he was called back. The King of Northumbria came to him with some churchmen, and they told him he had been elected Bishop of Lindisfarne and they asked him to come back and serve.

There's a Victorian painting of the king and the hermit. Cuthbert wears a dirty brown robe and has one calloused hand on a spade. The king is offering him a bishop's crosier. Behind him, monks kneel on the sands and pray he will accept it. Behind them are the beached sailboats that brought them to the island. The air is filled with swallows. Cuthbert's head is turned away from the king, he looks down at the ground and his left hand is held up in a gesture of refusal. But he didn't refuse, in the end. He didn't refuse the call. He went back.

We head out because the emptiness negates us. We leave the cities and we go to the wild high places to be dissolved and to be small. We live and die at once, the topsoil is washed away and the rock is exposed and it is not possible to play the games anymore. Now I am exposed rock. Like Cuthbert, I have been washed clean. What do I see?

I wonder if she misses me. I wonder if she remembers me. I wonder if she can walk yet, or speak. Has there been a first word? Perhaps she needs me. Perhaps I should go to her. Would that be the right thing? How do I know what the right thing would be? I look at it now, I have a year's distance, I look at it now and I see myself illuminated from behind, walking away from light and into light. I was the questing hero and the treasure would be mine, and when I came back with it, when I came back changed, they would see that change even in the way I carried myself as I approached over the hill. Everything about me was different now, they would see this and a great joy would rise up in them, and when I reached them they would welcome me back, wiser and better, a better person, and they would forgive everything. They would forgive everything and everything would be better, and I would be better. That was how it would work. That is how it will work, when I see them again. Yes. I am sure of it.

The storm isn't abating. If anything, it's getting worse. The gap is getting bigger, it's crashing around up there now, it's coming apart, it's all going to come apart and then what, then what? I'm going to have to go up there. It's dangerous, I don't know what might happen if this keeps up. It's not safe in here. I'm going to have to go up there. If I don't do something now, the whole roof is going to co

y eyes. I was lying wet wet through on wet stone slabs. It was dark. It was night. It was warm. There was no movement anywhere not in the yard I was lying in not on the dark hills around me not in the buildings around me not in the air. No movement and no sound. The silence was deep everything was silence.

There was pain everywhere there was so much of it that I didn't know what to do. I lay with my eyes open. My head was bleeding there was blood on my face. I felt that things were broken. Some of my ribs were broken. My left leg was numb where I was lying on it. I thought that was broken too. I lay still and thought about moving. I was scared to move but I was scared not to. I wondered what had happened.

Slowly I tried to bend my left arm at the elbow. It was trapped under me it was numb but it did move. I felt a great relief. I tried to move my right leg I bent it at the knee and at the ankle and it worked too. It hurt but it worked. Then I did the same with my left leg and my right arm. My left leg was hardest it was still numb and when I moved it a huge fire shot through my knee and up my thigh. I almost screamed. But it moved. I brought my right arm over my chest and placed my palm on the ground and I pushed myself up slowly with my right hand and my left elbow. As I pushed myself up I felt something in my chest give way. On the left side of my chest where I had been lying I felt something shift inside. I nearly threw up I nearly fell back down again and stayed down.

But I stayed up. I stayed up and then I pushed myself further until I had both hands on the ground and then I shifted my right hand back around to my right side and I slowly pushed myself up until I was sitting. The pain in my chest was enormous. Things were moving inside me which should not move I was sure of it. But I stayed up I stayed conscious I stayed alive. After a few minutes of sitting and breathing and willing myself to stay strong I shifted again over onto my right thigh. The pain in my chest was still there things were still moving around in there and now my left leg as well was screaming at me there was a shooting pain all down it and my left knee would not do what I wanted it to. I shifted onto my right thigh and I started to lever myself to my knees. My left knee wouldn't take any weight so I put all the weight on my right and now I was on all fours.

I turned my head to the left and to the right as far as I could. I felt the muscles or tendons in each side of my neck pulling taut as I did so. I seemed to be in some kind of farmyard. Behind me was a broken-down barn and to my right a wooden five-bar gate through which I could see a track leading down a small valley and out of sight. To my left was a stand of great silent trees huge in the stillness towering over the buildings. In front of me was an old stone house with its door ajar. I breathed heavily and carefully and then using all the strength I had left I started to crawl towards the door.

I could hardly put any weight on my left side at all though my left arm seemed to be working despite the pain. I shuffled like this I shuffled like a broken creature dragging my damaged leg behind me breathing deeply and steadily gritting my teeth moving slowly across the dark yard towards the door. Through the window I could see what looked like the dancing orange glow of a fire. There was no rain it was still and hot like summer though I felt it wasn't summer. I breathed in and out in and out I got into a rhythm of steady pain and slow movement as I shuffled slowly across the hard ground.

When I reached the door I pushed it open with my head and I crawled into the house like an injured dog. A fire was burning in an iron stove and the place was far too hot. I was thirsty I realised when I saw the fire that I was so thirsty. There was a mug of water next to a bed. I made my way over to it still crawling and I drained it. Then I levered myself up onto the bed limb by limb and I sat on the edge. I sat up as straight as I could which was not very straight because my chest would cry out if I tried to uncurl it.

I felt myself all over with my hands. My head was bleeding there was a long damp cut across my scalp above my left ear but the blood seemed to be slowing. I was wearing a shirt and jumper. I lifted them up to examine my torso. It was so tender that I could barely touch it. All down the left-hand side of my body were great bruises yellow and black. Across my chest running from just above my right nipple down almost to my belly button were five long scratches. The pain was intense but there was no real blood. Slowly I unbuckled my trousers and slid them down my legs. I feared what I would see but I had to look. My left leg was bruised and black and the knee bent at the wrong angle. As I sat I could feel it stiffening. There were scratches all over my legs but again there were no deep wounds.

– 25 –

What had happened? Whatever it was I had been lucky I supposed. I didn't seem to be dying. I didn't know what I could or should do with my battered body but sleep was all I wanted now. There was a dirty red sleeping bag on the bed and I crawled into it lay on my back closed my eyes and went into the darkness. I wonder how long I slept for. I don't know. I think it might have been several days. It was impossible to keep track after a while and in any case I was not trying to. I woke and went back woke and went back the tide was pulsing in and out in and out and in sleep the pain gave me dreams. I saw white stags and white wolves and black trees. I saw an island in a lake I saw the moon over a moor I saw fleets of ships in the sky. I saw a woman staring at me. I knew her though I had never seen her before.

It might have been a few days before I came round properly. It was never clear. I remember the dream that carried me back. There was a great tree standing on a hill there was a light around the tree and it had deep roots. It had great tall branches reaching to the sky twining around each other and its roots went down into the centre of the world where something lived and moved around them. There was a man standing under the tree there was something bright covering his head and he was moving towards me. There were birds around him all around him were strange birds.

I opened my eyes. It was light. Daylight. It was light and it was warm. The fire was out the ashes were cold but the room was hot. I lay there and I concentrated on what I could feel. I adjusted to my body and tried to re-inhabit it.

I was lying on my back in the sleeping bag. I must have been twisting and rolling in my sleep because the bottom of the sleeping bag was wound tightly around my feet and my lower legs. I lay on my back in the heat and I went through every part of my body systematically and examined its state. I started with my feet. I wiggled my toes and twisted my ankles around. They seemed to work as they should. I moved up to my calves I flexed their muscles and they both worked too though the left leg gave me shooting pains. Then the knees. I could bend my right knee, but the left seemed rigid and it felt wrong. There was a flaming arc of pain when I moved it and it would barely bend.

When I turned my attention to my thighs it was the same. I could tighten the muscles in my right thigh but my left thigh sent shooting pains right up into my abdomen when I moved it. Then my hips. I twisted them and they moved on both sides. On the left side

– 27 –

I could feel the agony of this movement but the fact that I could feel something felt like a triumph despite the pain. I was alive. I had not died in my sleep I could still move I was not paralysed. I flexed my stomach muscles and the pain in my left side was still intense. All through my abdomen was a dull throbbing ache.

I could bend my neck left and right though I still felt the pulling in the muscles when I did so. I twisted my head to both sides and it moved too. I rolled my shoulders I bent my elbows I curled and uncurled my fingers. It all worked. I opened and closed my eyes. My head ached a throbbing ache and constant. I was so thirsty and now I was hungry as well. It must have been hours maybe days since I'd eaten anything. I needed drink and I needed food and that meant I needed to move from the bed.

I looked around me. I was on a bed up against a wall on one side of what must have been a front room in an old farmhouse. The walls were of grey stone with some peeling paint and the floor was stone too great slabs of it. In the centre of the room was a wooden table and a battered old chair. Up against another wall not far from the front door was the stove and beyond that to one side of a window that looked out into the yard was an old wooden cupboard.

What would happen when I tried to cross the room? I remembered the collapse inside my chest that I had felt out in the yard. How was it now and what would it do when I got out of the bed? If I couldn't move now if I rolled out of bed and the pain was anything like it had been when I had fallen if my chest kept shifting inside me I didn't know what I would do. Something bad had happened to me some accident but I had survived it. I had survived these days in bed I had drunk and my body had slept. I felt better but I was still broken. I felt like I was floating above everything like I was floating above the ground like a spirit like mist over fields in the morning. Sometimes I had felt like I was floating above the pain. But now I had to move.

I rolled over onto my left side. I felt something shift inside me but I kept going. I swung my legs slowly down onto the floor still in the sleeping bag. I pushed myself up slowly with my arms. The pain in my head became worse I could feel the throbbing now I could hear it. Something was hammering on the inside of my skull. Pain shot down the left side of my chest and down my left leg. I pushed myself slowly up with my hands and I slid the sleeping bag down under my legs and onto the floor.

It was time to try and stand up. Things had been

slipping around inside me again as I sat up but they seemed to have settled now that I was sitting still. The shifting had not been as big nor as painful nor as fearful as it had been out in the yard. Perhaps I would come through. I swung my legs around gently to the head of the bed and I sat on the pillow so that I could balance myself against the wall as I stood. And then gently and slowly I tried to stand.

My left leg would not support me. The knee bent at the wrong angle again it bent outwards and my foot shook if I put any weight on it. But my right leg worked. I pulled myself up against the wall slowly standing on my right leg and putting as little pressure on my left as possible. The pain in the left side of my chest grew in intensity. But now I was leaning against the wall. I was standing.

I turned around so that my back was to the wall and I leaned on it. I had one hand supporting me on the head of the bed and the other still on the wall. I took breaths. Breathing hurt but I began to breathe deeper to see what my chest would do. I couldn't manage really deep breaths. If I tried there would be a great shrieking pain in the left side of my chest. But I could breathe. The pain in my head was worse now and the pains in my chest and my left knee and all down my left leg were real and terrible. But I found I could bear them.

Gently and nervously I moved my right hand away from the bed and over to the left side of my chest and I began to press. Everything was bruised. The five long scratches down my chest were beginning to scab over. They were deeper than they had looked. I worked my way systematically from the bottom of my ribcage upwards pressing gently on everything. About half-way up there was a sharp give in two of my ribs. I nearly fell over when I touched them. They must have broken. They felt wrong but I supposed they couldn't have punctured anything important or I wouldn't have survived. I could still breathe and I had not bled to death in the night. How did ribs work? I didn't know anything about medicine. Did they just heal? I knew that bones would heal themselves in time. Maybe if I didn't touch them they would recover.

I looked down at my knee. That looked worse. It had swollen into a great yellow and black ball and it felt like it was burning from within. It was splayed out-wards at an angle it should not have been able to bend at and I couldn't put any weight on it. How would I walk? Was it broken?

I didn't know anything outside the miracle of my

life. It mattered only that I was here. Here I was. Here I was alive and standing and breathing. Now I needed to eat and I needed to drink and I probably needed to do something about my knee as well. That was going to mean walking. That was going to mean walking from the bed over to the table and the chair and the cup-board in which I felt there would be food. By the cup-board on the floor was what looked like a jerry can of water. I could see that the can was about half full. The true power of my thirst hit me as I looked at it. I could not remember ever being this thirsty.

I pushed myself away from the wall as if I were pushing a boat out into a lake. I swayed for a moment and stumbled I went down hard onto my left leg and a great sheet of pain shot up through the left side of my body. I screamed and flailed my arms in the air to keep my balance and I rocked back onto my right side but I stayed upright. I steadied myself and then I began to walk. I had to put some weight on my left leg as I moved and every time I did I would screw up my face involuntarily and try to keep from crying out though there was no-one to hear me. I could have screamed to hell and no-one would have heard me but I would not let myself. I kept walking stumbling towards the wall. It seemed to take much longer than it must have taken but I got there. I collapsed in the chair and rested the weight of my upper body on the table.

From the chair I could just reach out and open the cupboard. In the cupboard I found a cracked china bowl of soft potatoes some dried beans in a plastic bag a loaf of bread a pile of teabags a packet of painkillers and two big bars of chocolate. When I saw the chocolate my heart leaped. Sugar and water I wanted sugar and water so much. I took out the bars of chocolate and the pills. I dragged the jerry can of water over to the table and opened it and poured water into an old blue mug on the tabletop. I drank and drank four or five or six mugfuls. I took four painkillers and then I unwrapped one of the bars of chocolate. I ate it deliberately slowly. I felt the sugar slide across my tongue and down my throat and set my body running. Then I drank two more mugs of water and sat in the chair at the table and breathed steadily and gently.

After a while the pain in my head began to subside and the throbbing died down a bit. The pains in my knee and my chest didn't change but they were less of a problem if I sat still. I decided that my chest would heal itself if I just left it alone. I didn't know if that was true but I had nothing else to tell myself. There was nobody here to help me and I could not go looking for help. Where would I go? I didn't know anything about that. Nothing was clear. I was here and this was my problem and that was all.

But I knew I would have to do something about my leg if I was going to be able to walk properly. A splint was the only thing I could think of. I sat at the table and looked through the window at the sky in the yard. It was pure white. The air was hot and muggy as if a storm was coming. Everything was still and quiet. I sat and thought about splints. What was a splint exactly and how did it work? As far as I knew I needed a stick. I supposed I needed a stick as long as my leg and something to strap it to my leg with. Some rope. That sounded right. There was clearly nothing like that in this room. If I wanted a stick and some rope I would have to go outside.

When I found the strength and inclination I hauled myself to my feet again and I got myself to the door the same way I had got myself to the table. I was mastering this slow and strange way of walking already. A body will adapt to anything. I got myself to the door and I swung it open and hobbled out into the yard outside. There was an impression of whiteness and stillness. It was hot out here as well. Hot and muggy and still and the sky was a uniform white across the farmyard and over the top of the silent ash trees and up to the moor. A ripped tarpaulin a steel ladder and several plastic bags lay in the centre of the yard. I turned myself around and looked up at the roof of the house I had been sleeping in. A sheet of corrugated iron was hanging off. There was a big gap in the roof.

It was so still. I stood in the warmth in the white warmth breathing. I had worked out just how much breath I could take in and ease out without my chest screaming. My breath was all I could hear. I stood in the centre of the yard breathing slowly and steadily surrounded by ripped tarpaulin and plastic bags. The door of the house was open and the sky was white. There was white everywhere. Things drifted into my head and out again. Words and offerings cravings and needs all of them tugging me around demanding that I follow them. I let them come in and roll out again roll on into the whiteness without me. I didn't know what any of this was. I stood breathing in breathing out watching it all come in and all roll out in the silence of the still trees and the empty weight of the stone beneath and around me.

In the barn on the other side of the farmyard I found a frayed stretch of blue nylon rope and a broken handle from an old broom or rake. I used the handle as a walking stick on my way back to the house and found it made the journey easier. Inside I leaned on the door until it closed and then I sat down on the edge of the bed. I wondered what I should do. Did I just strap the handle to my leg? I supposed it was that simple. It was slightly shorter than my leg and that seemed to be about right. But my leg would not straighten. It bent outwards at the knee and the knee would not bend without terrible pain.

It was agony. I tied the blue rope tight around the top of my thigh and then I wound it in a spiral down both my leg and the stick pulling it tight as I did so. I thought I was going to die it was so painful but I would not scream. This was my mission this was my pride I would not scream I would do this without screaming. By the time it was done I was sweating and shaking. I lay back down on the bed and hauled my splinted leg up onto the mattress. The leg was shaking and my hands were shaking but I felt heroic. Was I supposed to sleep with it on? I wondered. How long should it be on for? Was this right? Had I made things worse? I didn't know anything. But I looked at my leg and through the pain I could see that it was straighter than it had been. I hoped that was right. It was too late now.

I lay there letting the pain and the shaking subside letting the sugar run through me and the water do its work. It felt like morning. I had images in my head. Shapes but no names. People feelings fear and anger and shame and purity and wonder all of them making shapes inside me. The shapes came the shapes come the people come and go. I am coming and going rising and falling with all of it around me. I know so little here I know nothing. My name is Edward my name is Edward Buckmaster there are circles around me I am a stone dropped into a pool. Something has happened I am in pain I am still in pain. Someone is waiting for me where the moor ends. I think there is much that I do not see.

It would be impossible for me to guess how much time passed in this way. Every day was the same and this was how it had always been. Every day in this stone room with the table and chair with the cupboard and the window with the white heat outside and around me. I was here and perhaps had always been here or perhaps had never been here before but I didn't think much about it. I had my body to think about I had to rebuild I was being born again in the world retraining my muscles understanding my pain.

In time I developed a daily routine. I would wake

in the morning or what I presumed was the morning because when I began to think about it I saw that it was impossible to tell what time of day it was. It always seemed to be hot and light I never saw the darkness come or go and I had no watch so I simply told myself that it was morning when I woke. Every morning then I would lever myself stiffly out of bed. Every morning I would pay attention to the level of pain in my leg and in my chest and in my body as a whole. Every day on waking I was seized with a panic a kind of fear that the pain would be worse that something would have gone wrong in the night that I would not be able to move because if this happened it would be the end. But in fact every day the pain was either the same or a little better. I would lever myself out of bed and I would lie on the floor and slowly I would stretch and flex every part of my body until I felt I was ready to move.

Then I would open the door and I would go outside into the white heat. Every morning after I had stretched and flexed life back into my body I would step out into the air to remind me where I was to remind me of my life. I would take the jerry can with me and slowly I would hobble and shuffle on my splinted leg across the yard and through the wooden gate. As my confidence had grown and my body had come back to me I had begun to explore the place. The first priority had been to find water and beyond the gate and down the track I had found a place where a small stream pooled and the water seemed clean and fresh. Every day I would fill the can with as much water as I could carry. Then I would hobble and shuffle back up to the house dragging the can behind me and pour myself several mugs of it and sit at the table and drink slowly and feel the water echo down my throat and into my stomach because this was life. After that I would light a fire and heat water for tea even if I didn't want any. I would eat a little bread though not too much because I needed to ration it. I had no idea where to find any more food or how I would get there even if I knew. While it lasted I ate chocolate and every other day I would allow myself some painkillers if I needed them.

I would sit by the fire as it warmed willing it into my body holding my hands over it feeling the heat rise. I would make tea and drink it at its hottest feel it scald my lips my tongue my throat feel the life burning down into me. I would stand and walk around the room. All day I would try not to sit or lie still for too long. I had decided that I must train my body back into working shape. Making a fire tending the fire drinking water collecting water moving through the door out of the house back into the house in the white heat of the day and the white heat of the night. There was nothing else. Nothing seemed to change nothing seemed to move but every day I was sure my head was clearer every day I was sure the pain was less and less.

At first I started counting the days but I soon gave up. Perhaps it has been about three weeks since I opened my eyes out in the yard. This is my best guess. Three weeks of sleeping eating drinking collecting water walking slowly around the stone. Three weeks of the white heat that is everywhere three weeks of the silence. Three weeks of slowly gathering strength. I am lying here now on the bed but the splint is gone. I untied the rope and unwound it a few days ago. It was a risk but I think it has paid off. I can put a little weight on the leg now and the knee looks more like a knee again. I have been using the former splint as a walking stick because I still can't walk properly though I have come a long way. My leg is straighter though still not as straight as I think it should be. I still get headaches. It is still hot and white and quiet. There are no birds no sounds outside I hear nothing. I am sweating again as I lie here but that is because of what has just happened. I need sleep. I'm sweating and exhausted and the pain is beating inside my skull it is clawing at me trying to break free. I almost feel like I have relapsed. But it was worth it. Because today I found what I went looking for.

Let me go back. Six days ago I think it was six days ago I woke with what I supposed was the morning light. I got up slowly and eased my stiff body out of bed. I still seized up in my sleep and I still felt like a corpse every morning. I walked around the room a couple of times and I began to unwind. Then I walked to the stove and lit a fire to make tea. I went over to the door and opened it and hobbled stiffly out into the yard as I did every morning. The pain down the left side of my body was still constant. My knee bent in the wrong direction but at least it bent now. I thought my ribs must be healing. At any rate I was still alive. I stood in the yard and I faced the four directions in turn. The sky was still white it was still hot and the ash trees were silent. Above the farmyard loomed the great brown slopes of a moor. Some mornings I would stand in the yard and look up at the moor and feel it was my protector. Other mornings I would feel it was my jailer. Some days I refused to look at it at all.

The moor was an enemy this morning. It was watching me whether I stood in the yard or hid inside my room and closed the door. It was a great presence which held me down and I would not be held down anymore. I had been in this small world for so long circling the table circling the yard drinking sitting walking up and down. Everything was white and split apart and nothing was known. For me to be here. I could not stay here a moment longer. I had to go. Broken in this broken place I had to walk into the whiteness. I needed to see beyond. I needed answers I wanted words put to shapes I wanted a history. I wanted to name this place and all the things in it. It was enough now. There could be no more.

I decided I would walk away. I would walk to the town. I was sure there was a town somewhere and that it was not so far I felt I remembered this and I thought that maybe I knew how to reach it. I felt that if I left and headed down the track and just kept walking then my body would remember where to go. When I got to the town I felt that something would happen. There would be answers there. Things would become clear in the town there would be other people and questions could be asked. I would see familiar things for I had been to the town before I was sure of that. There were images there were notions of it. This place now it was caging me it was tightening around me there was no breathing here. Something would happen in the town.

And even if there were no town even if I got lost on the moor then at least I would be away from here. At least things would open up and begin to happen again.

I went back inside and made tea and drank it slowly. I ate the last of the very stale bread. The chocolate had run out weeks ago but I hadn't been hungry recently I just wanted to drink. My body craved water. I drank some and took the last of the painkillers. My headache ebbed and flowed but it never went away. Then I packed a jacket and a bottle of water into a rucksack that had been hanging above the bed and I strapped my boots on slowly and painfully. I couldn't tie my left boot tightly. I picked up the stick that I'd used as a splint and I walked out of the door into the whiteness.

Everything was white. It wasn't just the sky everything was white and new and washed clean. A new energy flooded through me new life came into me as I moved as I headed for the beyond. I went out through the farm gate and closed it and made my way slowly down the track outside. The muggy white heat pressed in on me as I walked. I stopped within a few hundred yards and took my shirt off and walked in my T-shirt. I continued downhill along the track. This was a test for me. I felt it was a long way to the town but a sense of direction was coming to me now a sense of where I was what this place was. Yes. I would have to climb the crest of the moor and trudge through rough heather. Up and over and down. I didn't know if my body could carry me but I would try this because the only other thing was to return to the stone room and I would not return there.

As I walked I felt the strange and awkward rhythm of my crippled frame. I was lurching down onto my left leg and supporting it with the stick then loping ahead with my right. I felt like a beggar on a slow pilgrimage but the result was an intense awareness of what I was. I could feel my body working or trying to work I could feel the muscles straining and how the bones knitted together and moved with the tendons. When I got to the stream I turned right and followed it up towards the shoulder of the moor. The climb was hard work. I had to stop and drink regularly. The heat didn't help. Halfway up the climb I stumbled over a rock by the stream and sat down heavily on it. I decided to rest. The sound of the stream was the only sound I heard. I had already got through half of my water and I was only a mile or so from the farm.

I continued slowly up to the tops and then I followed a peaty track through the heather. I was on a huge expanse of open heather moor now wide and brown and green under the close sky. On the horizon to my right I could see the moor climbing upwards and peaking in a high rocky tor. To the left of the tor the land sloped down and slid into a deep stone gully. I walked now in the rhythm and I didn't stop. I didn't want to break the spell. I could feel my head emptying but I didn't will it. I just walked and breathed and felt my legs jerking over the black track as I headed slowly towards where the other people were.

It must have taken a couple of hours for me to walk across the top of the moor following the black track and keeping to my rhythm. When I reached the point where the track began to descend I knew that I would make it to the town. I didn't know how I felt about that now. All of my questions seemed to have been swallowed by the heather and the sky but I kept walking because there was nothing else. Soon I arrived at a wooden gate where the rough footpath became a lane that headed down into the valley where the town was. I remembered it all now. I went through the gate and began to walk down the lane. Hedges of elder and ash and thorn grew up on either side of me and beyond them the heather and broom of the moor began to give way to fields of grass dotted with patches of bracken and bent, gnarled trees.

It was then that the silence really hit me. It had been quiet in the house and in the farmyard and up on the moor but this lane was stiller surely than a lane should be. There were no rustlings in the undergrowth there was no noise in the hedges or the trees. No cows no dogs no sheep no cars no voices close or distant. No animals at all and no birds either. I realised then that I had not seen or heard any birds since the accident. There was no life here at all. Nothing moved except me.

I kept walking. I felt it was perhaps a couple of miles now to the edge of the town. I passed an old church which I knew I had seen before. It was a squat medieval church with a square tower and a giant yew tree in its graveyard. I felt it was early afternoon though I couldn't see the sun to make any judgement. I wondered what would happen when I got to the town. I didn't know what I wanted. Suddenly I felt the need to explain myself. Perhaps I wanted to go shopping. I probably needed food though I wasn't hungry. Or perhaps I wanted to go to a doctor. There would be a doctor there. Perhaps I should show somebody my knee and my ribs and the scratches on my chest perhaps I should talk to somebody about everything that had happened. I kept walking. When I got there I would know what to do.

And then I found myself outside the church again. I found myself coming down the lane to the church again. I found myself coming down the lane from the moor to the exact same point where I had been perhaps twenty minutes before. I stopped and looked around me. I didn't understand what had happened. As far as I could remember you just followed this lane down and it went to the edge of the town. But here I was outside the church again and I was sure I had passed this way already. I sat down and drank some water. It was still hot. I didn't know how I had managed to get lost. Perhaps I had remembered wrong. Everything was still so unclear. I had probably got it wrong taken a wrong turning. I set off again down the lane towards the town paying attention this time to where I was.

It happened again. After another twenty minutes or so I found myself coming back down the lane towards the church. I was puzzled now and angry too. What the hell was happening? I was angry with myself. I had thought I would manage this trip. Now it looked like my legs could do it but my mind could not. What was going wrong? Where was the wrong turning I was taking? I couldn't remember taking any turning at all. Up the lane was the moor and down the lane was the town. It seemed straightforward. Surely it was straightforward.

I tried it again. I tried it twice more and the same thing happened each time. For the fourth time I ended up coming down the lane towards the church. I was sweating now it was hot and white everywhere and so quiet and I was furious. I was furious with myself I was furious with the place I was furious with the fucking church and the fucking moor. I was almost out of water. I felt like crying and I wanted to sit down.

I decided to go and sit in the church and get my breath back and consider. It would be cool in there and silent and I could drink my water. There might be a tap somewhere. I could fill up my bottle and try again. I went through the lych gate and down the tree-lined path to the church's main door. I tried the iron handle and the heavy wooden door opened. When I walked in the cold stillness enveloped me. It was a relief. There was nobody else there.

I went and sat in the front pew before the altar. I drank the last of my water and I breathed slowly until I began to cool down and calm down. I watched the quiet light coming in through the stained glass window. The church calmed me. The ancient silence the cold stone the smell of dust. It was a well of nothingness and I drank from it until I was as still as the air it enclosed. I sat there for perhaps twenty minutes.

Nothing happened at all there was just the great stillness of the old stone cradling me. When I felt like I had recovered I went exploring and behind the altar to the left I found a small room with a sink in it. I filled my bottle. Before I left I bowed my head. You have to bow your head to something.

The heat and the whiteness and the silence descended on me as soon as I opened the church door again. I stood in the centre of the lane and looked and listened. Nothing. I wondered what to do. I had thought this lane was asphalt but now I saw that it was dust. It was the fourth time I had stood here and I was tired. My legs were aching and my head was throbbing.

There was a field by the church which I felt had once had ponies in it. There were no ponies now. I stood by the silent hedge and gazed into the empty field where the ponies had been. I had no idea how I kept getting lost. I had been returned here again and again. My mind was clouded so much had been shaken. Now I wondered if I had the strength for another attempt to find the town. What if I got lost again? Time was passing and my body was aching.

If I headed back now over the moor I would probably make it back to the farm. If I lost myself a few more times on the way down to the town I didn't know what I would do tonight. Perhaps it was best to go back to the house to sleep and try again tomorrow. Maybe tomorrow it would not be so hot maybe tomorrow I would remember which way to go maybe tomorrow things would come together again I would not be floating like this above the ground my mind floating above the ground like a spirit like a will-o'-the-wisp like something from the otherworld.

And then I saw a movement. In this still white empty place there was a shift. From the corner of my eye perhaps a hundred yards or so down the lane I saw something come out of the hedge bank and cross the road. It was big and long and dark. It seemed to be a couple of yards in length it was low to the ground and it was black. It was some kind of animal. It seemed to come out of the thorns on the top of the stone wall that edged the lane and jump down onto the road. I turned towards it instinctively I swung around but it was faster than me and by the time I was looking in its direction all I caught was its long blackness disappearing into the hedge on the other side of the lane.

Whatever it was it had seemed to walk on air. It made no sound. I stood there hot and floating above the ground and I tried to pull my mind around to get my mind to fix itself onto what it had seen and to consider it. I was tired I was dazed it was a strange day but this had been real I thought. Some big black animal had crossed the road ahead of me.

I stood there for some time. I waited for minutes I don't know how many but I heard no sound and I saw nothing more. Whatever it was did not come back there was no sound no movement anywhere. But where could it have gone? On the other side of the hedge bank into which it had seemed to disappear was a patch of open moorland. There was broom and heather and bilberry all over it and small thorn trees and scrub but I had not seen it cross the moor. Was it still in the hedge? Had it followed the wall on the other side of the hedge bank out of my sight? Was it somewhere in the scrub or the heather? Was it waiting for me? Was it dangerous?

I started to move. There was nothing else to do I couldn't stand there all day I had to move and I wanted to go home. My leg was so stiff now my side was so sore I had walked too far today I had pushed myself too hard. I loped forward slowly. I kept listening but I heard nothing and I saw no movement. If I had seen it what would I have done? If some monster some great black animal had come out of the hedge in front of me what would I have done? I could barely walk by now. But nothing came. I kept moving forward slowly towards the place where it had crossed the road.

I reached the point it had crossed at and I saw then that it had not been in my mind. There were marks on the road. They were faint but they were there. They were the prints of a big animal. They were so far apart. I squatted down with difficulty and I reached out and touched one. I brushed my hand across its dust and it was as real as the thing that had made it. Something had crossed here. Something had walked ahead of me and here were its marks.

I was afraid now. It had been so big. But there was nothing here it had gone. I could feel there was nothing here. If anything had wanted to pounce on me I supposed it would have pounced by now and I was so tired. It felt like my last reserves of adrenaline my last reserves of strength had shot through me when I saw what I had seen and now they were ebbing away. It was all I could do to keep upright. But I knew the way home from here I knew that at least. There was nothing to do but start back. I turned and I began walking back up the lane.

It took me hours to get back. It was probably late afternoon or early evening when I arrived. My legs were throbbing and my head was throbbing. I drank a couple of pints of water but I wasn't hungry. In any case there wasn't much food left. I had no interest in food I was exhausted I was broken and tired to my bones to my cells but I didn't want to sleep. All I could think of was the animal.

What had it been? It had been black I was sure of that and it had been big. Long. It had left footprints. What had it been? On the table in the stone room was a small pile of books. One of them was a guide to the wildlife of the British Isles. I sat down and flicked through the section on mammals. There was nothing that matched what I thought I had seen. It was far too big and long and black to have been a badger or a fox or even something rare like an otter or a pine marten. It had been nothing like any kind of deer. It had been steady rather than nimble and low rather than tall. There was nothing bigger. Humans have been in this place long enough to have killed off anything that threatens us. There are caves underneath this land with old bones in them. Wolves hyenas elephants rhinos lions they were all here once when this place was a forest and their bones still rattle around down there on the black banks of the underground rivers when the storms are in spate. But they are all gone now. So what had I seen?

In the same book I looked up the tracks I had seen on the road. I knew before I did it that it wouldn't help. They had been very faint prints on a dry dusty road and it had been hard even to make out their shape. I was pretty sure of their size though and there was nothing in the book that resembled them. Like the thing itself the prints were too big to fit with anything we had managed to name and number and draw a picture of.

The only other possibility I could think of was a dog. It could have been a Labrador or a sheepdog or even a wolfhound. Something big. But it hadn't moved like a dog and what little I'd seen of it had seemed to be a completely different shape. And when a dog bounds into a hedge it usually makes enough noise to scare off every living thing within thirty yards. And dogs don't just disappear they are too clumsy and noisy they come leaping back out again with their tongues flapping. And if it was a dog where had its owner been? I hadn't seen anyone. All dogs had owners I was sure of that.

It was not a dog. It was not a deer or a badger or a fox. It was not a muntjac or a pine marten or a mink. It was something else. It was something that was not in any of the books and I knew this even as I went through the ritual of crossing out the possibilities to placate the insistent demands of my forebrain. I sat at the table with the wildlife book open in front of me and I felt little shivers of fear crackling through my body like electricity. It seemed like a fear much older than reason. It was as if something had been triggered.

I was tired as hell. I stumbled over to the bed and pulled myself into the sleeping bag. I was seizing up again. I would need sleep. I was going to go back tomorrow. I wanted to see it properly. I would not try to go to the town again. I had no interest in the town. I couldn't think what had interested me about the town at all. There was nothing for me there. The search was somewhere else. I would not go to the town I would go again to the lane by the church and I would sit quietly behind a tree or in a hedge or behind a wall and I would watch and wait until I saw it again. I would see it again and then I would know.

I woke the next morning with a deep irritation inside me. I opened my eyes and some anger was coiling and uncoiling itself in me like a great worm. I felt it in the pit of my stomach I felt it rise through my navel it burnt along the lines of the scratches down my chest. I couldn't tolerate my physical pain as I had the day before. The pain in my ribs the pain in my knee the pain in my head which never stopped all of it angered me it twisted me around a stick and held me over a fire. I was shifting inside my own body it was like some giant itch I wanted to throw it all off and run. I wanted to scream I wanted to burst out of my small self into the world ablaze I closed my eyes and saw my mind straining at the bars lashing out at the world all of the smallness and stupidity. I saw it all finally crushed all the people flattened the glory of the end of it all. Skyscrapers falling oceans overcoming the defences the silence descending. I didn't want this stillness now I didn't want this warm white stillness I wanted to be the wild man naked in the rain the raging monkey tearing at the flesh tearing at the fucking red flesh. I wanted to rage smash things throw them break through tear it all up bite bite bite until all was torn all was hanging down loose and dripping all was pain all was broke.

I lay in the sleeping bag and watched the crescendo rising and falling fermenting and turning around and around. I didn't know why it was here or what it had come for. Maybe I had walked too far yesterday maybe it had just been too much. I got out of the bed slowly and moved across the room and when my injured leg caught on the chair I kicked the chair hard across the room and cracked one of its legs. That made me angrier and I swore furiously at myself. There was no food left in the house apart from some soft sprouting potatoes but I still didn't feel hungry I just wanted water. The water level in the jerry can was low and that made me furious. Why the hell hadn't I filled it up? The whole thing was just fucking ridiculous look at me here in this fucking place it was fucking ridiculous who was I what was I doing I was sick of it all I was so sick of it. I was sick of myself and my broken body and this giant itch this giant coiling worm I wanted to burn it all down take myself away jump from the roof and fall. That would be a response. That would be some fucking response.

I sat on the cracked chair and breathed deeply until I was calmer. The giant worm was still in there but I tried to let him be. I took the jerry can and went out of the door into the yard. It was as warm and white and silent as it had been for weeks. I went through the gate and down the bank of the combe to the pool where I collected my water. The pool was clear and still and I filled the can from the little trickle of water which became a waterfall when the rains came. I was surprised at how low the stream was.

I went back into the house sat down and drank four or five cups of water. I wasn't hungry but I thought I should eat. There were a couple of crusts of stale bread next to the sprouting potatoes. I couldn't be bothered to get the stove going to cook the potatoes so I just ate the bread. I nearly gagged on it. It didn't do anything about the itch. I still wanted to explode and take everything here with me. I still had no idea why.

But I had work to do. It didn't matter how I felt I had work to do. I packed a couple of the books into the rucksack I filled the water bottle I put on my boots and I walked out into the heat. I followed the same path I had followed the day before up the stream and onto the moor over and down again towards the lane. The day before I had turned inward as I walked. I had felt every step I took I had experienced my own motion the warm air upon me everything that I was. Today I had no interest in myself. My only interest now was in the land around me. Still nothing moved still I heard no birds. If anything moved at all then I would see it instantly. But I saw nothing all the way to the church.

Of course there was nothing in the lane. I knew as soon as I arrived that I was wasting my time and I was angry with myself for coming. I had seen an animal. Why would I see it in the same place twice? I stalked up and down the lane impatiently looking for signs but I found nothing. I couldn't find the prints I had seen yesterday. I was hot and angry. I took out my water bottle and drank some of it. I breathed deeply again.

My chest rose and fell but the itch clung on like a tick.

I kept going. As I had crossed the moor I had made a plan. I would be systematic about this. I was going to find this thing. I walked down the lane for a further half-mile looking for tracks. Then I climbed painfully over one of the hedge banks and followed it up again on the other side of the hedge looking for marks or shit or black hairs or anything at all. I did the same with the hedge on the other side of the lane. Nothing. I fanned out over the fields then and I walked each field on both sides of the lane. At my slow pace it must have taken me a couple of hours to scan the area around the spot where I had seen the thing. I walked around all the fields over the scrub and the sparse heather around the bent trees over the grasses and the plantain. Nothing. No prints no shit no hairs. No sound no sound at all anywhere.

I wanted to go into the church. I wanted to be entombed by the cold stone to get out of this heat to sit in an empty pew and ease myself. I wondered if I could work the anger and irritation out of me and have the old stale air of that place carry it away through the stained glass and out into the whiteness. I wanted to go in but I stayed outside. I had come here to watch. I sat down with my back against the trunk of the ancient yew in the churchyard. From there I could see out onto the lane to the place where I had seen it and for some way on either side. If it came back here I would not miss it.

The yew must have been centuries old it was hollow at the centre and the wood I was leaning on had been twisted and gnarled by the ages. Its green needles were thick above me its berries scarlet. I drank more water. I said nothing to myself or to the tree or to anyone I could dream of or think about. I just sat and watched the lane and the hedges and the fields and nothing happened for hours or what I thought must have been hours. I had no watch and so time was nothing not even a concept time was nothing and nothing happened. When you sit like this you realise that nothing has its own energy that it moves that nothing can *happen* like an event or an episode. Nothingness extends itself emptiness moves and when you stare into it things happen to you. I sat with my back against the yew and I looked across the churchyard wall over to the lane. Inside me the worm was still coiling though it was moving more sluggishly since I had settled down.

At the end of the hedge where it curled around the corner of the lane and disappeared out of my sight was a tree. It must have been fairly young it had a thin trunk and its slender angular branches hung over the lane. There were no leaves on it so it was hard for me to tell what it was. Maybe a beech maybe an oak. If you sit looking at anything for long enough then everything else fades from your vision and all you have is what you are staring at. I was staring at a small knot above the biggest branch on this tree. Its trunk was black and it was bare in the white heat and suddenly I saw what terrible things trees are. They sprout up from the Earth they reach out in all directions they reach out for you they will smother you they will never stop growing and dividing and colonising. They are so fecund there is no stopping them. Chop them down burn them they always come back up they stretch to the sky these thin green fingers they are indescribable. They are just waiting there waiting everywhere for us to fall and then they will come back and they will grow over everything they will suck it all in and take it up to the sky in their thin fingers. Their roots will wrap around all that we were and our lives will rot down in their litter and theirs will be a silent Earth of roots and leaves and thin grasping and there will be no place for us in their world at all.

Then I remembered a man who would go out every morning and look at his trees. I didn't know who he was or where I remembered this from but it felt like a memory and it came to me as I stared across at this tree in the lane. He was an old man he wore a tweed jacket and a flat cap and he planted trees. Perhaps they were fruit trees. I remembered that this man whenever I passed he would be in his garden walking slowly between the trees shuffling between them and inspecting them looking at every leaf turning the blossoms over smelling them sometimes. What goes on in the head of a man who looks at trees like that? He did it for years perhaps he had always done it perhaps he is still there doing it now. What went on in the head of someone who could do that same circuit every day for years forever? Why couldn't I do that? Who was he that I was not? Today the thought of his circuit the thought of his silent circuit of the trees filled me with horror. How much I hated trees how much I feared things that grew. I was surrounded by trees surrounded by things that grew surrounded by this horrifying green abundance and it all wanted to swallow me and it was so silent so slow it spoke no language I could understand. How I hated it how I hated it and how I wanted to run.

I stopped looking at the tree. I found myself back in the churchyard leaning against the yew but now the church seemed to loom behind me like some presence. Now that I was aware of it I couldn't put it beyond me I wanted to turn to look at it to make sure it wasn't moving towards me coming to claim me. Now the church felt like a threat. What if God was a tyrant? The Bible's God is a tyrant he destroys worlds because people won't obey him he flies into rages and floods everything he burns down cities he slaughters children he hands down rules which must be obeyed by all and for eternity. He sent his son to die for us and he demands our gratitude for this though we never asked for it he demands that we gather in squat stone buildings and sing his praises if he is not to flood and burn us again. God the Father of all the men who feared their fathers over the centuries all the men who built up his church and who feared their fathers and whose sons feared them.

And outside the church where they go to worship God is god humming in the air god who is the air the unmeasurable and strange thing. This god who is not in books and did not live or die and is not a father or a mother and will not be obeyed and will not be denied. god who is the molecules and the air and the trees this forcing light this strange light roaring out. Before words before language before thought before speaking everyone must have been able to see this clear white light. Now it is all clouded. But you can make the cloud fall away or it can fall without you and then you can see again what is underneath the trees the soil the ideas the opinions what was always underneath them. The light has nothing for you it makes you no promises. It is in the small things it is in the tiny things we walk over and past the tiny things that run the world and we never see them because we believe we are running it ourselves and we are walking past to lay our claim on it first. The beetles the bacteria the earthworms the centipedes the viruses the mycelium the seeds lying dormant in the soil waiting for us to burn ourselves out. For the meek shall inherit the earth.

I was a stranger here I could see it now I was a foreigner an invader an immigrant and they were turning on me. The trees the hedges the beetles the things that live in the soil they were turning on me hissing at me they wanted me out they wanted me gone. The anger inside me had shifted and now it felt like a fear like a great anxiety. I felt all alone in the world I knew there was nothing here for me nothing at all. A bottle of water a walking stick a pair of boots was all I had between me and the trees the grass the gods and the gravestones and they all wanted me gone they were coming for me. This was their world and they would take it back they would take it back from me soon there would be no lane here no church no paths I could see the future and in it was nothing but trees nothing but the things living in the trees and in the soil a great silent green orchestra spread across the whole of the world. I had walked out too far. I had walked to this lonely place and now I was surrounded and they would eat me.

I had to leave. I had not seen what I came for but I didn't want to not now. It was ridiculous it was impossible it was nothing. I raised my stiff body up and I began to walk back up the lane towards the farm. I carried myself across the moor as fast as I could but it was not fast I leaned on my stick and my rhythm was awkward and all across the moor I felt there were things in the heather surrounding me coming for me I was being watched some great force was just behind me shadowing me stalking me and I couldn't turn and look back. I just kept walking with this fear this anxiety inside me I didn't know what it was but I walked I had to walk and I didn't look back.

It was some time in the afternoon when I got back home. The first thing I did was to light a fire. It was still hot but I wanted a fire. I needed something else in the room with me I needed some other life something else that moved I needed a friend out here alone surrounded. I needed a friend and in the dancing of the flames and the warmth of their movement I had something at least that understood me and that I could speak to.

The next morning was different. I awoke to a sense of trying to hold on. In my sleep I had been moving and trying to hold onto things and there was one more thing to hold onto and I knew that I had to hold onto this because if I couldn't I would fall and then it was over. I wanted it to be over I wanted to fall because then the struggle would stop and the struggle was so tiring everything was so tiring. But I had to grab onto this thing it was my last chance that was the compulsion I wanted to fall but I had to hang on and I was flying then and I woke.

I lay there staring at the gaps in the roof and remembering. Everything that had happened yesterday seemed ridiculous. It was clearly ridiculous. The fire was out and the room was warm and outside the window was the whiteness the stillness and the silence and what had been happening? There was no fear now and the fear I had felt yesterday seemed so far away that it was as if someone else had felt it. It was nothing to me. Trees and a church it was nothing to me and there was nothing to feel about it. This morning I felt calm and level and inside my mind I saw a whiteness that matched the colour outside the window. I levered myself out of bed and in my movements as I crossed the room and pulled on my clothes there was a stillness as well. I wasn't thinking and everything was like crystal. Here I was and out I would go again and that was the way things were and what was there to be afraid of what was there to feel about anything at all?

I sat at the table and poured a mug of water from the jerry can and drank it slowly. This would be my routine now. I would rise when I woke and dress myself and sit and drink a mug of water and look out of the window at the whiteness and everything would be still. And then I would slowly put on my boots and take my stick and pack my small bag and walk out and I would cross the moor and go to the lane and wait for as long as I needed to. I had all time if time was even passing. This would be my routine until I saw it again. What did I want to see and why? I sat and I drank my water and this wasn't clear to me but it didn't seem to matter. Not very much seemed to matter. There was an emptiness all around me and in me. I was sure I cared about a lot of things but I couldn't think what they were. What was the great work of my life I wondered and was it underway?

It was a quiet day. Every day was a quiet day now. I walked steadily down the track across the stream up and over the moor. I reached the lane with no expectations. All was still. Today I didn't enter the churchyard instead I sat outside with my back against the stone wall on the grass verge by the track. I took out my bottle of water and I placed it between my legs in front of me. I put my rucksack on the ground next to me and I folded my hands on my lap and I waited.

Everything was benign. I remembered the fear I had felt yesterday. I looked across at the same tree I had been looking at then but I couldn't imagine how it had stirred those feelings in me. The huge whiteness of the sky curled over me like a dome and seemed to sit with me. Nothing would happen here I knew that now I had known that as soon as I had sat down. Nothing would happen here even I would not happen here. I would only sit in the whiteness with nothing around me. But I felt like I was happy to do that all day and maybe all year. It was so still. Nothing flowed through me or around me. Life was nothing and this was how it should be I felt as if this was how it should always have been. I would just sit here.

I had brought no food because I didn't have any food I only had water now and anyway I still wasn't hungry. Food seemed like a form of pollution. I drank water and this was fine. Perhaps I sat there for a couple of hours. I knew I would see nothing and I was happy about it. Nothing was fine. Nothing was good. This was how it was meant to be.

And then it changed suddenly just as it had changed the day before. I took a swig of water from my bottle and I closed its cap and put it down on the ground before me. When I looked up again I saw nothing that I had not seen before and yet none of it looked the same. This time I wasn't frightened. Instead I felt despair settling slowly and gently down upon me. There was no panic and no urgency. There was nothing to run from. I accepted what I felt almost immediately. But there it was: a gentle, strong, loving despair enveloping me. I felt like the nature of things was laid quietly out before me like the wares on a market stall. For a moment the world cracked open and I saw myself as the wild creature I was as one caged wild creature among billions as atoms as meat as animal as prey. As another small victim the world would not mourn because the world did not mourn it just went on. The wheel of blood and sperm and death and life kept turning and none of it needed me none of it knew me for there was no me and never had been. I saw the abyss open up and I knew I would be swallowed by it and I knew that everything in my world everything I was and everything I thought and felt and cared about and refused to care about had been carefully constructed only to help me survive any glimpses I might have of this.

What was all this? Everything was so silent and still and sad. There was nobody here but me no creature no noise and it seemed clear to me in this moment that it was driving me insane. How could it not drive me insane? The silent hot white place and everything I had been drifting away on the stream so far that I could no longer see it. I accepted it all. It was fine. I had no desire to change it but at the same time I was clear what was going on. It was horrible. I was so alone. I was so alone and that was all there was and would ever be and there was nothing to be done about that now.

I got up and I turned and walked to the church-yard gate. I walked down the path and I pushed open the church's wooden door which was ajar. The building was cool and close and immediately I felt different. The despair seemed to be hanging in the air outside like mist. Inside the building it dissipated. I sat on the very last pew at the back of the church and I held my cold water bottle in my hand like a relic like something that connected me to a world I felt I was floating away from. The whiteness came through the stained glass window at me. To make a window like that. To make this altar and these carvings and these windows to make a spire that points to heaven and to put one in every settlement in the land. What did you have to believe to do that and would it dissolve what was hanging in the air? Did beauty dissolve what was hanging in the air could beauty dissolve anything or was that a lie? Did people make windows like that anymore or did art die with God in the twentieth century? If a tower doesn't point to heaven why build a tower? If your hands are not folded in prayer what are your hands folded around? As the white light walked through the many colours did it bring the despair with it and would it settle on me again? What did this window tell me as the light came through and this unknown saint rose in red and gold and pointed his staff at me? That there is art and there is god and everything else is a waste product.

I sat in the pew and I breathed and it was fine. It was all fine. Everything was as it should have been. How could I ever have thought otherwise? I liked churches.

Eventually I rose and went back to the door which was still ajar and closed it behind me. Outside the despair was still drifting gently around in the air. This was a waste of time. It was obviously a waste of time to sit here waiting for something which would never come. I didn't mind that I had wasted my time. I didn't feel that I had anything better to do. But I didn't feel like wasting any more of it so I put my pack on my back and headed up again onto the moor.

On arriving back at the farm the first thing I felt was a strong urge for a drink. But not water. I wanted beer or whisky or wine but of course I had none of these. I filled up the lone mug on the table from the jerry can and drank more water instead. I couldn't remember the last time I'd wanted a drink. Now I wanted to be drunk. I wanted to be pissed for days. I wanted to fall onto the floor and have visions and wake up sick. I wanted to pick up a dirty woman in a bar and fuck her upside down in a car down some filthy lane. I wanted to smoke weed and fly and curse and sing I wanted to run screaming through neon streets I wanted to sit in dark corners in underground clubs I wanted to puke everywhere and bounce off the walls and go to sleep forever. All of this whiteness all of this silence.

I drank two more glasses of water and took a number of very deep breaths. It became clear to me what I needed to do. I needed to create a system. A system would lock out the fear and the silence and the despair and the whiteness. I needed a curriculum to follow. This sitting this aimless sitting day by day it was getting me nowhere and there is madness in nowhere. That is where real madness is to be found in the middle of nowhere sitting in the whiteness unthinking that is where it all breaks open. Nobody can survive that. You need to run from that when you see it coming over the hill.

I would make a plan. I was going to find the creature and I was going to be systematic about it. There was no point in just hanging around where I had once seen it. If there was something if there was some big creature and if it was living around the moor it would be moving about. It would probably have a big range. It must be living somewhere. There would be somewhere it went at night a cave or a barn or a tree or a hole. It probably had a circuit on which it hunted. There were probably places it liked to go at different times of day. It would have habits. I would learn the habits and I would use them to track it down. I would see it and then I would know.

There were two maps of the moor on the table with the books. I took them from the tabletop and laid them out on the floor so that they fitted together like a jig-saw. On one of the maps I found the church and the lane and I circled them in pencil. Then I started draw-ing. I sat on the warm stone floor cross-legged with my mug which I filled up at intervals from the jerry can and I measured and drew. Time seemed to sink into the moment as it does when you're not thinking about it. Time didn't pass it just coalesced around me like jelly. I had no notion of how long I sat there. It didn't get darker outside but I hadn't seen darkness for days. It was light when I went to sleep and light when I woke up and because I had no watch I didn't know how long I slept for and because I didn't know I didn't care. I sat there in the even light with my mug and my pencil and my two maps and I drew.

When I had finished I had what looked like an uneven pencilled spiderweb connecting the maps. In the centre of the web where the spider would sit were the lane and the church. Around them I had marked a grid comprised of eight mile-square sections. Within each of these squares I had drawn a series of lines which divided them further into smaller areas. Around these eight squares I had marked a further sixteen which I had also crosshatched internally with the same regular lines.

It was a simple geometrical system and the plan that went alongside it was simple as well. The square in the centre of the map covered the place I had been for the last three days. I had already walked most of this area in going to the lane and coming back again and exploring the fields around. I had satisfied myself that there was nothing there. I didn't know if the thing I had seen would ever come back there but it was the only place I'd seen it. So I would treat it as the centre of the area to be explored and I would systematically explore the land around it. Each day I would select one of my marked squares and I would walk along the crosshatched lines within it until I had systematically walked the entire area of the square. I would walk slowly and quietly and I would look for any signs of the creature. The next day I would do the next square in the same way.

In eight days I would have covered an area of nine square miles centred upon the lane. If I had still not seen it again or come across any sign of it by this point I would proceed to the outer circle and explore the next sixteen squares. That would take me just over two weeks. If I'd still not turned up anything I would start again in the centre of the grid where the lane was. This way I would cover an area of twenty-five square miles in slightly less than a month. I would repeat this cycle until I found it.

This was a good system. This would work. I stood up stumbling slightly and steadied myself on the edge of the table. My left leg was numb again as it so often was when I sat still for too long. My lower back ached. I took another sip of water and looked down at my map. I had no desire for alcohol anymore. The despair had gone. It seemed like a strange mirage now and I couldn't imagine where it had come from. This would work. I was pleased with this. It was a net that would close around whatever I had seen. It would bring it to the surface so that I could examine it. I would see it again and then I would know. I would start tomorrow.

The next morning I was in a city. It was boundless it seemed to stretch to all parts of the horizon. It looked like a Third World city it was full of slums all of the buildings were strung together with corrugated iron and plywood and bits of old crate and cardboard and barefoot little black children ran around in the streets laughing and kicking deflated footballs and open sewers ran down the edges of the roads and none of the roads were paved. There were women washing clothes in the river talking together as they worked there were men trudging home over the hill in flip-flops and shorts walking back from some pain they had been paid for. There were skinny dogs with their ribs showing lurking in doorways. The sunlight was blazing down. There was hunger and there was poverty but the place was full of life people knew what they were hemmed in by and nobody was lying to themselves about what they could be and nobody had come to tell them what they weren't and so they just lived.

I was walking through this but nobody saw me. I was an alien here. I came down to a lake and the lake was clear and some boys were jumping naked from a rickety pier into the water screaming with laughter and pulling themselves up again onto the wooden struts their naked black bodies shining in the sun. One of them saw me and pointed and laughed and another one of them hid behind his bigger friends and I walked down to them on the pier and I saw that I was tall and white and angular and covered in cloth and a stranger to my own awkward body and to these children who were at ease in themselves. My pockets were full of money and I wanted to go across the lake but nobody would take payment. Can you help me across the lake I said to the boys and one of them said to me I will teach you to swim sir but you must take those clothes off. And so I took all of my clothes off and I stood there tall and white and pale and hairy amongst these small sleek black boys and the boy I was speaking to said you must jump in there sir and he pointed to the water.

And I didn't hesitate I just jumped in and my head went under and it was freezing and the water was all over me and I surfaced and looked at the boys and they were all lined up along the edge of the pier looking at me. And I said I can't swim and they said you can swim sir if you choose to but there is nothing else we can do for you now. We are glad that you came back. And I could see the other shore of the lake and there were rushes growing and a small boat was hidden in them a small wooden boat and I could swim and I started across the lake and things tugged at my ankles as I moved there were things under the water. I kept swimming.

The morning routine was the same every day now and I had come to enjoy it. Wake up clothes on two mugs of water pack bag boots on pick up stick open door step out into the white heat. It was as white as quiet as empty as ever. As before I headed across the stream and up the shoulder of the moor and over it towards the church and the town. But this time I stopped before I went through the gate that led down off the moor and into the lane. I took out my map and I walked until I was exactly in the corner of the first marked grid. The lines that crossed it back and forth on my map were not related to any footpaths or track-ways on the ground. They were just lines on the map and in my mind and I would follow them as best I could. I would move slowly and steadily. There was no hurry. I had all day.

I decided that the challenge was to follow the lines precisely. I would walk the straight lines I had drawn on the map no matter what obstacles I came across on the ground. This would keep me going. It might be fun. Who knew what I would find. I would watch the ground on which I walked and I would keep my eyes on the horizon and anything that happened I would see immediately. Nothing else moved there was no other life there was only the hot and the white and so anything that came to me I would see.

On the map this was an empty grid. Some of the others had features in: ponds streams woods cairns paths. But this was an expanse of heather. The only landmark in this square mile was a giant's grave. I turned the words over in my mouth as I began to walk. Giant's grave. Giant's grave. To be in a land with giants' graves in it. Some great old menhirs fallen in on each other and what was beneath? To just walk past these things without a second glance and everything they once were.

I would love to dig down and expose the skeleton of a ten foot tall man with a bronze shield at his feet. Yes there were giants in the Earth it was all real all of it. All of the stories they told you when you were a child they were all true. Imagine that. Imagine if adulthood is the fairy tale and childhood is the reality. Imagine giants' graves all over the land and the motorways roaring past them and it is the motorways which are the romantic lies. Beyond the places you can walk to there is a field of buttercup and clover which rolls down to a river and that is where the life is that is the reality and here you are walking through a grey dream.

Within each square on the map I had drawn two sets of five parallel lines running from north to south and from east to west and crossing each other at intervals so that the whole thing looked like a chessboard. It meant that to cover each marked square I would have to walk ten miles. For the first mile I kept my mind entirely focused on my task. I felt the muscles in my legs move as I walked across the heather and I felt the still hot air passing my ears. I walked at a medium pace. My left leg still spasmed with every step. The ground was springy and the heather was woody and dry. There was nothing but peat and heather not a stream bed or a combe or a stunted tree. This square mile of moor was a great rounded shoulder of heather and in the middle of it was the giant's grave.

The giant's grave was my goal. I was going to walk in complete stillness and silence until I reached it. According to my map it would be about three miles of walking until I got there. Three miles of sameness three miles of heather. I picked up the pace after a while. I was getting bored. There were no signs of anything up here. No big animal would be up here surely it was too exposed there was nothing for it. There were no holes in the ground nowhere to hide nothing to eat. If it had walked here I would not have seen any tracks beneath the heather anyway. But I kept going. At any moment things could change and I had a system and I was going to stay with it. I had seen something and it must be somewhere. I would find it.

I reached the giant's grave after what must have been an hour or so. It consisted of three great old slabs of granite one lying horizontal and the other two resting at angles on top of it. All three stones sat on top of a slight mound. I took off my pack and put it on the ground. I took out the water bottle and climbed up to the highest point on the stones and sat down. I surveyed the landscape. I was at the highest point on the dome of heather which sloped down towards the edge of the moor. There was a kind of heat haze around the edges. I could see the tower of the church beneath the trees where the lane was. I couldn't see the town. It was silent. No bird sang. I drank some water.

It was the heather that brought the falling man back into my mind. The smell of the heather the roughness of the purple buds the texture all of it spread around me and seemed to raise something and I remembered a man who fell over a man who had some meaning to me. I felt it was a memory. I was young perhaps. He fell and he didn't rise. Or perhaps he didn't fall perhaps he jumped but he went down and didn't come up and that was everything then there was nothing after. I don't know what this is. Perhaps when we die the world just ends. Perhaps everything stops when we do which means that we are everything. I wondered: what if each of us is everything? What if everything is concentrated in every part of us? All of the essence of everything is in every tiny cell and every particle. So nothing can survive without anything else which means that when one thing dies everything dies and then it is all instantly reborn again in a new form.

What if we are not all sharing this one world but instead every one of us creates their own world and that is true of everything that is? It is true of you and me and every other human and it is true of every other living animal and every bird and every fish and every tree and every mollusc and every bivalve and every arthropod and every virus and every fungus and every germ floating in the air and all of the rocks too all of the grains within them everything constantly dying and the universe ending with every single death and starting again at precisely the same moment so that there is no time as we think we know time there is only this constant ending and this constant birth?

Or what if it is all about kindness? What if that is the secret? What if everything is about kindness what if that is the great kōan that the world offers up to us? What if this is the big secret what if this is the answer that once everyone is kind to everyone else and to themselves and to everything that lives even the rocks and the rivers then the world will end and we will be done? Or what if everyone is given just one tiny task in this life what if we come into the world with our own tiny task but we don't know what it is? Maybe our task is to write a great book or speak a certain word or love a certain person or discover a certain thing or walk a certain street or kill a certain creature or dream a certain dream. What if each one of us has to find their task and then complete it and if we don't complete it we are born in another form and given another task and everyone and everything will keep being reborn in every form there can ever be and given these tiny tasks to find and complete and only when all of them are done will everything be done. Maybe then all the suffering ends maybe then the game ends and we find out what's really going on behind the scenes and who the gamemaster is.

Everything is rising and falling expanding and contracting the universe grows and shrinks a million times every second. Or there are eleven universes all running in parallel and whatever you are doing now you are doing in all of them. Or there are hundreds of these things hundreds of these universes thousands of them rising and falling expanding and contracting beating like great hearts entwined. Sometimes it all falls away and there you are beating with all of the other hearts with every heart in every universe beating and beating. You are a cell in the heart you are part of it and it cannot beat without you. You are hurtled into the void and then catapulted back towards the beginning again. It takes a billion years and happens a million times a second and here you are and there is the void and it is everything and it is coming for you and it is fine. This is just how it should be. Everything is the same anyway.

I drank almost all of my water up there on the stone. It was too hot. One bottle wasn't enough. I still wasn't hungry. I slid down the stone I felt the roughness of the granite beneath my hands. The stone was warm like it was alive and it comforted me after all the heather. I felt a kinship with these stones. Lying here like abandoned lovers like sleeping elephants like the dead with all of their sadness they comforted me. Everything was so still so silent so white. How long had it been since I had seen another creature? The stones felt like creatures to me. I wanted to throw my arms around them and nobody was watching so I did. I leaned on the biggest stone and I embraced it and it seemed so long since I had been embraced and I wanted to be. I wanted arms around me I wanted to be comforted. I remembered arms around me now I remembered someone who did that and for a second I saw her face and smelt her and saw what was in her eyes for me and then it was gone and all I had was stone. I needed something I could slip into because this was too much now this was all too much. I needed a heart to speak to mine but there was no heart there was only rock. I wanted to stay here but there was nothing here for me and so I had to keep walking.

It took a few hours to complete the grid. I saw nothing. No evidence of any creature no evidence of anything except heather and one dry stream bed and in the end the footpath that took me back home again. But that was fine. I had completed my first task. Tomorrow I would complete my second.

In a wood a man rose from a bed of leaves by a pool. They were autumn leaves dead and brown and the man was brown also and covered in hair. There was thick orange fur all over his body. There was a drumming sound in the forest all around him it was the rain the sky had opened up and had woken him from his sleep. He knelt and looked up to the sky. He tilted his head up and opened his mouth to receive the rain. The rain was falling over everything in the world. The surface of the black pool was dancing with it.

Something was different the next morning. I supposed it was the morning. I felt like I'd slept for a long time. It had been a hard day yesterday. But something was different and when I had climbed out of my sleeping bag and moved over to the table for my morning mugs of water I realised what it was. The air was cooler. It had been so hot and still for as long as I could remember but today it was not so cloying. Through the window I could see that the sky was still a uniform white but I could see something else as well: tiny spots of water on the glass. I looked down at the area of stone floor directly under the hole in the roof and I saw that it was darker than the stone around it and that it glistened.

I went to the door and opened it and stepped out into the yard. It was still warm but nothing like as hot as it had become recently. And it was raining. There was a drizzle a slight fine silent drizzle almost like a mist descending. I could feel the drops on my skin the tiny drops of water but I couldn't hear anything. It was so fine such a fine drizzle and it was a joy. Something was happening. The sky was still alive. The ground in the yard was damp and when I ran my fingers across the door handles and the windowsills they were damp too. In the night a gentle rain had begun so gentle that I had not heard or sensed it. I hoped it would continue. I hoped the rain would get harder I hoped there would be a downpour and that everything would be washed away.

I went back inside feeling light. I realised how heavy I had felt for so long. Since the accident everything had felt like such a burden I had felt like something was clinging to my back but today I could step lightly again. I didn't know why. I sat down and drank three glasses of water. Today I would walk the second grid. Judging from the map it would be a more interesting walk than the day before. There were a couple of streams to cross and there were some hut circles with a ditch around them. It would mostly still be heather because everything was heather up here but at least something would break up the pattern. And today I would walk with a light step. It was fun. It would be fun. Everything was fun. Why not?

I packed and set off down the track along the combe. I packed quickly because I was eager to be out in the rain. With my rucksack on my back I stood out in the yard and I spread my hands out and I raised my palms to the sky and I stood there until my muscles began to hurt so badly that I had to lower my arms again. I stood there and let the fine mist fall onto my hands and my exposed forearms and I turned my face up and the rain fell onto it the fine thin rain. The rain was warm like the sky and it was beautiful. It seemed to bring life with it and it brought the lightness that I could now feel inside me.

I felt like skipping down the track I felt like dancing. I closed the gate and headed down the combe and I tried to skip I tried a merry dance down the track but my left leg would not stand it and I stumbled and fell. I fell onto my back and I lay there and laughed and felt the fine rain falling onto my face. How long had it been since I had laughed? It had been so long. I couldn't remember ever laughing in my whole life. Perhaps I never had. I lay there for minutes giggling and feeling the water settling on me. Was there any reason I could not lie here all day laughing in the fine rain?

When the laughter had run its course I lay there feeling empty and light. After a while I thought I should get up. I still had a job to do. I rolled over on my side to push myself up with my arms and I found myself gazing into the mat of grass and plantain and dock that grew alongside the track. I had never paid much attention to grass but now that I looked I could see that there were different kinds growing together entwined. There was a short wiry ferociously dark green kind and there was a kind with a long pale green stem with white seed heads at the end and a shorter kind with what almost looked like bright orange flowers on the top. There was every shade of green there were oval red seeds on tiny white stalks furring out from long stems there were flat blades and serrated needles everything was down here.

All of these grasses wove into the plantain and the dock and together they made a forest and looking at them from down here I saw them as trees I saw them creating a canopy. This was the whole world down here and I walked past it every day sure that I knew what the world was. But maybe this is where life was really going on. We blunder about with our heads in the clouds with our hearts in outer space and here is life going on amongst the woven grasses and it doesn't care about us and it will be going on long after we have burnt ourselves out. I could lie here all day and look at this I thought. I could lie here all year and look at this and perhaps if I did that I would learn something because up until now up until this very moment in my life I have never ever learned anything at all.

Then as I lay there about to begin the laborious process of standing up I heard a noise. It surprised me so much that I started. I was so used to the silence out here now I was so used to the hot white silence. I had seen and heard nothing since my accident except the thing in the lane. Nothing had moved nothing had spoken there had been no sounds at all. And yet now as I lay here in the fine drizzle under the white sky I distinctly heard a sound above me high above me. It was the sound of a bird. A skylark. A skylark singing up above the whiteness somewhere its high song its chatter rising and falling. It lasted maybe ten seconds and then it stopped abruptly and the silence returned. But I felt even lighter then. The sky was alive and something else was singing. Something other than me could still sing in the world.

I got myself up still feeling light and I followed the path over the moor as I had for days heading towards the designated grid. I felt now like my body was floating with the lightness. I felt happy. Had I felt happy before? I couldn't remember but this felt like happiness to me. I was light and floating I had seen the grasses and heard the skylark and here I was just walking. Perhaps I would see the thing today. It didn't feel like it mattered so much now. All I wanted to do was put one foot in front of the other. Perhaps I could just do this forever. Perhaps all my trials were over.

I was walking over the tops now and I felt my feet through my boots I felt every bump in the ground I felt the roots of the heather through the springy peat. And as I walked as I steadily moved I suddenly realised that I was not the owner of my feet. These were not my feet. They were not an extension of me. They were me. I was this foot and I was this hand I was these fingers I was these eyes. This body was not a vehicle carrying this mind around. Everything was me.

It is so hard to put into words into these clumsy words that say nothing. But the shift was real and total. I knew that I was not the owner of my body. I was my body. I nearly fell over in surprise. I kept walking and feeling both the feet touching the ground and feeling the knees bend as I moved. But now everything in the world was different. I came up onto the high point of the moor and I saw the lowlands fading off into the haze. Now I was this body everything was me and the sense that my mind lived in my head and that my trunk and limbs served it broke down and kept breaking down. Now I was my body but I was also what my body walked upon. I was the grasses all of the different grasses and I was the peat of the moor and I was the heather and the skylark I had heard and I was the thing in the lane and these were not ideas they were not concepts they were not thoughts this was just how it was. I was everything. Here and now I was everything that was and had been and I was everything to come.

I stopped walking. I stood still in the middle of the track and I surveyed the landscape around me and I understood that the eyes which did this had lived a million times before. The way I scanned this horizon was the way the horizon had been scanned by my ancestors fifty thousand years ago as they walked the savannahs with spears between their toes. They had made me. I had learned it from them. Everything my body did the way I curled my fingers and bent my elbows the way I turned my head when I heard a sound. I had learned it from them and they had learned it from the apes before them and the apes had learned it from the fish and all of us had come through this together. Everything led up to me and everything I was would lead beyond me there was this great chain and I was a link in it. The past and the future they were nothing they came together and parted again and everything was rising and falling and swirling around everything else.

I felt like I had fallen down a hole into a thousand years ago. I looked around me and everything was much older than I was. I didn't see anything so much as feel it. I felt I was in a wood and I could smell smoke and there were people around and maybe dancing. Carts were moving. Wooden carts. There was talk and I didn't understand it though the words were familiar. There were buildings made of wood and straw. There was a wooden pole and a group of men sitting around a fire and one man standing before them raising his arms. It felt like a ceremony but everything was happening on the other side of a fine sheet of gauze or through a two-way mirror and here I was just standing as if I were apart from it and yet I could see it. I was there and I was here I was just passing through and I seemed so small in it that almost I could not bear it. I felt like I was fighting off some huge emptiness just beneath the surface of everything I had ever pretended was real. I felt like I was breaking apart and I wanted so much to break apart and yet I resisted it. I so wanted to be broken into pieces but a fear was rising within me.

Then suddenly the fear gave way to a great calmness which flattened out all of the emotions within me made them white like the white sky. A great indifference came over me. I thought: I don't care about anything. I don't care about anyone. I'm sure there are people I am supposed to care about but I do not. I don't care about myself because I don't believe in myself. I don't care if I'm alive or dead or what happens in the world or what the world is or what comes next. None of it interests me. I don't care about this lack of interest. I'm not happy or sad. I don't despair I don't feel joy. I just am. I don't care about anything and because I don't care I have become free.

I came back into myself then. I came back into my body and onto the moor and I kept walking along the track. Here I was again out on my search with my pack on my back and my map with the gridlines on it. Here I was with my plan. And yet everything had changed. All that day as I walked the lines the calmness stayed in me the great whiteness and everything I had seen.

What I now knew about myself it stayed there and it would never leave me again. I walked the gridlines dutifully and saw nothing. No scat no hairs no marks no prints. I sat by the hut circles by the faint raised mounds of grass that marked where people had lived when this had been a town five thousand years ago. I heard nothing and saw nothing. I drank water. I walked my ten miles and then I headed home.

It came just when I had stopped looking. I was loping awkwardly along the thin black peaty path that wound its way through the heather. I was tired and I was thinking of my sleeping bag. On the way down back towards the track that led home I had to pass a wood high up on the shoulder of the moor. The wood had a wire fence around it. The edge of the wood with the fence was perhaps half a mile from me as I moved down off the moor towards home.

As I walked I caught a movement from the corner of my eye and I turned towards the wood and there it was. The thing that walks. It was long and low and dark and black and it was moving along the fence line. I couldn't see it distinctly through the drizzle. Almost as soon as I saw it it disappeared from my sight. But I got a better view than before and I had been right I had been right all along. It was not a dog or a deer or a fox or a badger. It was a long low dark animal with a thin curling tail that it held above the ground as it walked. Its motion was smooth and cool. I didn't see where it went. Into the woods I supposed. But it was real. I had been right. It was real. It was real and it walked and I had seen it again.

I was sure there would be no point in following it but I went anyway across to the edge of the wood where I had seen it. There was a scent in the air I was sure of it a sharp hard musky smell. I wasn't frightened this time there was nothing to be frightened of. I walked all along the fence line peering through the trees look-ing for movement between the trunks. Every time I fancied I saw something it turned out to be nothing. I looked for footprints but there were no footprints. I was so tired and yet I was floating with this now flying with it. I had been right. It was here. Again I had seen it again it had come. I was closing in.

When I woke the next morning a white horse was staring at me through the window. It was all white with a white mane. The end of its nose was grey and pink. It was just standing there staring at me curious. The muscles in its flanks and legs twitched occasion-ally. I could see its veins and sinews under the skin. It just stood there and looked at me with its dark eyes. Of course it was beautiful. I jumped on the horse's back and held tight to its mane and it ran it ran down the field it leapt over clover and buttercups. We jumped a hedge and then another we crossed more fields we saw no people there was nothing we just kept going until we entered a forest.

It was a deep dark tangled forest and we rode for days and days. We never stopped he kept running he was not tired and I held on and I shrieked for joy and the air ran across my ears and my hair. We ran and ran for days and weeks without stopping until we came to a great clearing of grass and bluebells and there I slid down off the horse's back and I lay on the ground and I looked up at the sky and breathed. The horse came over and looked down at me as I lay and I saw that he was not a horse he was a deer a white stag a white stag with golden antlers. And then I remembered that there were no forests anymore that you could not ride for days anywhere that you would be stopped by fences roads shops cars people that no horse could take you to this clearing now that there were no horses anyway. I sank into the ground then and outside the window the only whiteness was the sky and there was no whiteness in me and I was heavy.

I wonder if every animal is a spirit. That rabbit you

saw on the road the dog you live with the birds on the feeder in your garden the spider that hangs in the corner of your bathroom. What if they are all spirits sent to you and how you treat them is what you are. A thousand ant spirits in a nest and you pour boiling water onto them and what does that make you? Do you kick your dog or stroke him and give him a biscuit? Maybe your choice shapes the world and everything in it. Maybe that's the secret. There has to be a secret.

I felt tired the next morning tired and dirty and old. I sat at the table drinking my morning mug of water and thinking about the creature and suddenly I felt an overwhelming need to be clean. How long had it been since I had washed? I couldn't remember. Perhaps I had never washed. I needed to clean my body. I couldn't let the creature see me like this. There had to be some dignity. If I was not clean it would never come. There was a yellow plastic tub in the corner of the room which had probably been used once for collecting something from somewhere. Now I took it outside into the yard. The drizzle was still coming down. I went back into the house and brought out the jerry can which was two thirds full of water and I poured all of the water into the plastic tub. I put the lid back on the jerry can and took it back inside. Then I stood by my bed and took off all of my clothes. I left them in a pile on the floor and walked outside and stood in the bucket.

The water was cold and astringent it bit into my toes and ankles and widened my eyes. I squatted down and began to scoop armfuls of water up and scrub them into me. I scrubbed my hair my face the back of my neck my chest. I scrubbed every inch of myself all of the parts of me that had not been touched for so long that smelt acidic and old I scrubbed them I poured water over them until the water in the bucket was brown and greasy and I was washed clean. Then I stepped out of the bucket and poured the dirty water on the stones of the yard and watched it pool and puddle and snake away. I left the bucket there upside down and went back in to the house and sat naked and wet at the table and drank one more glass of water and watched the fine drizzle drifting slowly down onto the stone floor and the stove.

I looked down at my body. It was pale and knobbly and cream-coloured. The five long scratches that ran down across my torso were still clearly visible though they had scabbed over long ago and were now more like brown pencil lines. The left side of my chest was no longer red and swollen but it did seem to be a different shape to the right side. My left knee and lower leg seemed permanently bent at a different angle from my right. But here I was. This was me. I wanted to run up onto the moor like this naked and wet and greet the thing. I could run forever this way with nothing to encumber me. The thing would understand me like this it would know me this way. I was an animal wet from the watering hole clean now and ready.

I sat there dripping onto the floor and sipping slowly at my water until I was nearly dry and then I put my clothes back on. I only had one set of clothes and it had not occurred to me until today how much they stank. The thing would smell me a mile away when I went looking for it. I would have to wash them. But not now. This morning I was going out again.

I was going to abandon my plan. I had known the moment I saw it again outside the wood that things must change now that I must be flexible that I had been gifted another offering and that I had to respond. So today I was going to go back to the wood. It must be living in the wood or maybe hunting in it. I was getting close now I was zeroing in and I wasn't going to let it escape just for the sake of following some pre-conceived pattern. I was going to be thorough in my search and I was going to find it I was going to see it I was going to know. I had a feeling about this wood.

A creature like that this was the kind of place it would live it was the kind of place it would hide.

It wasn't far from the house to the wood. I made my way steadily and quietly up the shoulder of the moor with the familiar tor to my right over on the horizon. The wood was shut in by a wire fence with barbed wire along the top. There was a padlocked iron gate. There were ash trees and poplars and birches all around the edges and further in it was mostly yew and larch and spruce with a few oaks and ashes that looked older than the rest.

The first thing I did was to walk the boundary line of the wood outside the fence starting at the point where I thought I had seen it. Nothing. No prints this time even along the part of the fence where I was sure I had seen it walking. I kept examining the twists of barbed wire in case any hairs had been caught but there were none. Of course I heard no sound and I saw no creature. It wasn't there not now. Why would it be? Why would it stay? Why would it wait for me?

I climbed the fence carefully and stood inside the wood and listened. Silence the same silence that had held me for so many weeks. No birdsong no rustling in the undergrowth no distant cars no voices animal or human. Just my breathing and my footfall and the settling of tiny raindrops on leaves and on the woodland floor. I decided to walk the wood as if it were one of my grids on the map. I would walk in a series of straight lines from north to south and then from east to west and that way I would cover all the ground. Nothing would get past me. I was good at this now.

I began. I walked slowly from one side of the wood to the other and then I walked perhaps fifty yards to the side and began down again in the opposite direction. At one point I saw what I thought might have been a footprint of the kind I'd seen in the lane but the leaf litter on the floor was so thick and damp that I couldn't be sure really what I was seeing. Apart from that there was nothing. I walked this way north and south north and south for perhaps an hour and then I came to the edge of a deep pool of water. The pool felt old. It was long and narrow and it looked deep. Its surface was still and black. Long thin reeds and yellow irises grew around the edges. It reminded me of somewhere but I didn't know where.

I made my way down to the edge of the water until the ground got too wet for me to continue. I love staring into water. I looked down into the black depths but I saw nothing not even any insects moving on the surface. The whole thing was like a great old scrying mirror. I looked into the water and I was in a flat wooden boat making my way across it and there was nothing around me but the sound of the water. But I was not in control of the boat something else was in control of the boat and in control of me and all of the people. I was making my way across water but I didn't know where I was going and I didn't need to because what I wanted was not important now. I was a tool I was an object a means to a creation. I lay down in the boat the back of my head rested on the hard flat wooden planking and I looked up at the sky and the sky moved slowly above me and where I was being taken was no longer my concern.

There was nothing in the pool and there was nothing by the pool or around it. I walked the whole perimeter of the water I thought perhaps it might come here to drink but I saw nothing. So I continued with my plan. I walked the whole wood along my north south lines and then I turned and I did the same thing from east to west. Nothing. It was not here. Not only was it not here but there was no evidence that anything had ever been here even in the place I had clearly seen it the night before.

I made my way back to the gate out of the wood and I clambered over the top of it. I stood looking up at the long shoulder of the moor against the white sky. It was becoming clear to me that when I looked for this thing I never found it. I only ever saw it in passing when my guard was down when I was tired and hungry and walking away. My system didn't work. I dropped my rucksack to the ground took out my water bottle and drank half of it on the spot. Then I shouldered my pack again and I made my way up the moorland slope the way I had walked yesterday.

Something dropped into me the minute I walked clear of the wood. Something changed. Now I knew that the search would always be fruitless now I realised that for days I had had this tightness in my belly this great knot like a fist clenched inside me and I felt it begin to loosen. My bowels uncoiled themselves my stomach turned to jelly and a strange calm spread from it through the rest of my body. I dropped my pack onto the heather and sat on the ground. I leaned back against a rocky protrusion and let my gaze wander across the woodland past the wire fence up to the tor across to the gully. I felt the fine drizzle on my face and hands. I saw how damp my boots were. I was not going to look for it anymore. Looking for it didn't work. I was just going to sit and let my mind wander. There was nothing else.

I suppose I was there for a long time and in all that

time I barely moved my body. I was afraid that if I moved the fist would clench again and that I would be the solid old tree the metal pole the coils of wire wound tightly the solid thing that could not feel. As I lay against the stone with my pack next to me I felt like I was melting into the ground and this was good. I thought I would probably stay here forever. I had come here for this I was certain of it now.

And then as my gaze wandered towards the wood I saw a movement. At one end of the wood was a line of thin birch trees twelve of them white and upright and still in the misty rain. I looked towards the trees and it stepped out and walked slowly along the front of them. Perhaps it was fifty yards from me. It walked slowly along the line of the trees and then it sat on its haunches. It looked around as if it were scanning the horizon but it did not look at me and I felt relieved about that. But I saw its eyes. It had yellow eyes. It was a huge black cat with yellow eyes. It was bigger than I was. Perhaps it sat there for a minute and then it raised itself and walked calmly back into the birches and was gone.

After that everything was movement. I ran home or tried to. I stumbled hobbled tripped all the way home with an enormous joy welling up inside me from where the fist had unclenched. I had seen it! I had seen it I had seen it! It was a cat! A bloody big cat! It must have been the size of a tiger or a puma or a cheetah or something. What was it doing here? What would a big cat be doing here? How did it come out of the trees when I had walked through the whole wood and seen nothing? What was this? All of this what was this it was nothing. All of these were just words to me but this had not been words this had been so much more than words.

I almost fell back into the yard I was breathing so heavily there was an intense pain and joy throughout my body. My left leg was swimming in its own world my ribs were heaving I was sweating. I sat heavily onto the upturned yellow tub I had washed in before I left. I had a terrible headache again my headache had returned but the joy was overwhelming even that. A big cat. A big black cat! Jesus.

I was so tired. I am so tired. I want to sleep but what if I sleep and when I wake the joy is gone? What if I sleep and when I wake the vision is gone? What if I forget it in the night? What if it turns into words again? I looked so long for it I worked so hard for it I had wanted to see it so that I would know and now I have seen it but I know nothing I know less than I have ever known in the world. All I have now is questions. Questions and this great joy that is singing that is howling and crashing in me. I cannot even go inside now all I have is what is living in me here in this thin rain.

I wonder if I could explain this to anybody. I can see it now in my mind I can see it in my head the picture of it sitting there scanning the world looking around with its yellow eyes. And in my head too another picture a picture of a woman a woman and a child. A mother and child. A young girl a baby girl. I can see their faces. They are watching me they are scanning the world for me. I know them. Here it is now. Here it is. There we are now. There we a

s no god and god is everywhere. everything is breathing so what is the complication here. all these questions there are no questions. here is an earthworm here is the yellow flower of the broom here are my feet on the ground sometimes i find it hard to see them. i move them but i do not know how. god is the sound of a cat in the cloud. the cat god. i have not seen a tree for days. i would like to lick the clear water droplets off the leaves of a rowan. i will walk i will walk on. the running is the pain the running from. i will walk on.

listen.

there is a noise outside right outside.

there.

a scream.

it is loud and sharp and long and it tears me from my sleep. it is close. it is very close. i sit up in my bed in shock and i look around me. the shock runs in me like water runs.

the sound hangs in my ears. it was a scream. it was a shriek a howl. it was close as close as if it were coming from outside the door. right outside.

something is outside the door.

i sit up and i go to the window. outside there is cloud everywhere deep rolling thick grey fog. i can't see anything. i go to the door and i open it and the cloud rolls in. i slip my feet into my boots and i step outside onto the stones of the yard. it is mountain cloud it is sodden and weighty and it seems to move of its own will. it swirls and clusters and creeps about it writhes and coils around me. i can see the shape of a wall dimly perhaps a building nothing else. everything is grey and white and close.

the noise comes again. it is a scream a howl. it is very close.

it is right here.

i am glad that the people are gone. i don't think i have ever seen any people at all. there is a memory of them. now they are gone and there is no biting no climbing over there is no running from them all just to be. there is only the cloud and the wet grasses here and the sound. the sound and what is that sound.

the first scream came from my right i am sure of it. i am standing still in the cloud in this yard outside alone and now the scream comes again and this time it is in front of me is it closer i think it might be closer.

i wonder what is above the cloud. perhaps an aeroplane.

this time the sound is to my left. it is painful. i can hear it breathe after it makes the noise. now i hear it again now it is behind me.

it is circling me.

it is circling me in the cloud.

now i hear its footfall on the stones. i am frightened i am terrified. i am calm.

i am very calm i am on an aeroplane above the cloud. i am sitting over the wing and i can look out at the engine and i have my family with me my wife and children then as i look out i see the engine explode in orange flame and the plane collapses to one side and flips over itself and begins to tumble and scream from the sky. of course everyone is screaming and crying and things are flying all over there are trolleys and bottles and people flying all over we duck our heads my family and i we cling to each other and i tell them how much i love them and i hope it will be quick for my children. after this there is a safety demonstration.

the flight takes about four hours. i don't like flying.

i am very calm. yes i am enjoying this. the sounds the thing circling me in the mist. but now the sounds have stopped. i am standing very still here i am not trying to hear but i can sense that the sound will not come again i can sense that it is leaving or has left me.

yes. it has gone.

i stand here for some more time. i was right it has gone its presence has gone i can feel it. there is just the cloud now and it is empty and quiet i am standing outside in this yard and there is this cloud. when you are here in the cloud you are inside you are inside the life of the world. when you go into the house and shut the door you shut yourself outside then there is only you and the dead things you have made into shapes. inside is outside and outside is inside. if i were not so stupid i would have seen this years ago. wherever i have been.

i walk a few yards to my right to where i guess the thing was and i squat down and i scan the stones. even the stones as i squat down are hard to see in this cloud. but there we are. there are prints. footprints. there are the footprints of a big cat a big black cat a big black cat with yellow eyes. i remember this.

there is a small black cat in a big house it is hiding under a stuffed sofa. in the house there is a woman we are two sides of something. i walk through a door and she smiles at me hello beautiful she says i missed you i missed you too i say she puts her arms around me i remember this warmth. she puts her legs around me fucking in a bed can you imagine. animals fuck under the sky under the stars in the rain fucking in a bed it is disgusting all of our disgrace is here. there is no disgrace in a cat there is no disgrace in anything that walks on four legs that does not have fingers which dig into everything and take it all apart.

my fingers are wet they are damp everything is damp. i run my fingers across the prints on the cobbles the prints like a darker impression in the damp of stone. i run my fingers around the edge of the stone look at the shape of this look at the square shape look at the rounded edges someone chipped this someone carved it a man in cotton and coarse wool with scratched clogs and a lined face he made it and laid it down. he went home every night to a small brick terrace and washed the dirt off in a tin bath by the coal fire in the front room his tiny sparrow wife heated the water for him he drank too much because of what he carried but nobody would listen and anyway he could not say the words. nobody remembers him. imagine if nobody remembered me i would be so happy.

i stand and i turn around i look in all directions and in all directions there is cloud. there is no sound now i feel bereft i have been abandoned i have been left where has it gone my cat. why does it not want me anymore. i have seen it i have heard it and it has come for me so why am i still empty why am i so empty why am i in pain here. why did it come to me and then leave me alone. i am so frightened of what I want.

pain. my leg doesn't hurt my ribs do not hurt i remember all the pain and now as i stand here i can feel that the pain is gone all of it. how strange. i bend my left knee i bend my right knee they bend together the pain is gone my body is a pillar of light but my soul is empty and my mind is crying out to be filled. why did it leave me why did it come for me and then leave me again. how will i ever find it in this cloud.

this is a lonely place and cold.

they looked after me once once they looked after me. everybody was horrified they wanted to save me they wanted to get me out but i was happy there everything broke down and i was nothing and i have never been happier all of the sheets were so clean. now i am a pillar of light now i am alone and there is nobody to love me. i would like to be in there again with all of the others treated like all of the others.

when they put you there you don't have to pretend.

my hair is damp everything is damp and god i am hungry i have suddenly realised how hungry i am. i am famished i am hollow my stomach is crying out how long is it since i have eaten have i ever eaten. i turn i go back into the house and i close the door. inside the room i go through the cupboard and the drawers and all of the surfaces there is nothing here there is nothing at all. there is a can of water and a mug on the table but there is nothing to eat. now what am i to do about that. in this place in this cloud hungry and alone with nothing i have no money and where would i go if i had money when i can see nothing. i look for food for days but there is nothing and i grow weak. there is nothing growing in the yard there is nothing in the weedy garden behind the house and i grow desperate i try to strike out across the moor but i can't find anything i can see no paths i don't know where i am going in this thick cloud i wander and i fall and stumble and now i am waist deep in the bog and there is no getting away. the yellow water soaks through me the acid stench of the peat is a cloud around my mind i am too weak to pull myself out i sink into the bog and am mummified and they find me in five thousand years and academics build careers around the mystery that i represent.

when they built the stone rows and the stone circles the barrows and the avenues the climate was different here they could grow different things what did they grow i wonder wheat perhaps grapes mangoes cherries cheese chocolate i am so hungry i need food. maybe there is food in the garden. i pull open the door and walk around the back of the house to where there is a vegetable garden i have to feel myself around the walls of the house with both hands because the cloud is so thick. in the garden most of the soil on the vegetable beds is overgrown with cleavers and young red brambles and bindweed. i get down onto my hands and knees and i work my way along the beds and in the second bed amongst the curling goosegrass i see potato leaves i grasp the stem of the plant and pull it out and the roots come up with one tiny potato hanging onto the bottom. i put it down beside me and dig into the soil with my hands and turn over four more small tubers they have thick dark skins but they are hard and fresh. i dig all around the hole in case there are more but i turn up nothing i keep looking through the beds and in the next bed i find another two plants with another nine potatoes between them it is a feast i am so hungry.

i spit on the smallest potato and rub it across my

trousers to get the soil off then i bite it in half and i chew on the half that is in my mouth it is bitter and wet someone once told me that green potatoes have cyanide in them this potato will poison me i will be wracked with stomach pains in three minutes' time and i will lie here clutching my guts and throwing up but it will be too late i will die in the cloud here and nobody will find me for weeks. then two hikers will come up the track to the house looking for water a man and a woman in their twenties he has dragged her here she is a city girl she does not like this but she wants to please him and he senses this and so he holds her in contempt and soon after they will split up because they found a dead body in the overgrown garden of an abandoned house and this was not something they were built to take the weight of. i should be patient i should take this potato into the house and boil it and mash it with all the others i love mashed potato i used to eat it all the time with sausages or meatballs and frozen peas and gravy i expect something like that anyway and i would say that was enough for me. i would give anything now for a plate of sausages. i wish i were a cat that could hunt through the clouds for meat.

why did it leave me i want to see it i want it to look at me with its yellow eyes my cat. it has never looked at me i want it to see me. when i can look into its eyes then i will know.

the potato is disgusting my mouth is cracked and dry like glasspaper why did i eat a raw potato what a stupid thing to do. i gather up the rest of the tubers clutching them to my body to stop myself from dropping them and i carefully follow the wall of the house around to the door and i go through the door and shut it. i will light a fire and heat water and boil the potatoes and mash them. i drop the potatoes onto the tabletop where they roll about and come to a rest i find some paper in the bottom of the cupboard and twist it up and put it in the bottom of the stove i break up some dry sticks lying next to the stove and pile them in a pyramid on top of the paper. then i look around for matches. there is one matchbox and it is empty. i go through all the cupboards i look in all the corners i look everywhere there are no matches and there are no lighters i can't light a fire. i'm starving and the cloud is pressing in and the table is covered with muddy raw potatoes and i can't light a fire. i am furious about this to be here in all of this i kick the stove so hard that i bruise my toes on the solid black iron then i lunge at the tabletop pick up a potato and hurl it through the window. the glass smashes with a delicious sound for a second i feel guilty and expect to be told off but then i realise i will never be told off and i pick up another potato and throw it through the window as well. there are twelve potatoes left i pick them up slowly and carefully and i aim using all of my concentration and i use the twelve potatoes to knock almost all of the glass out of the window frame. when all of the potatoes are outside in the cloud and only tiny knives of glass remain embedded in the cracked putty i have a sense of pride. now the cloud is curling into the room.

i hate potatoes anyway i don't have time for potatoes. now i have broken the window there is nowhere to hide everything is outside and inside at once everything is in the cloud. there is no reason to be in here there is nothing in here for me there has never been anything in here for me. i want to look into its yellow eyes.

i look down at my feet. since i was woken by the scream i have been walking around with my boots unlaced i bend down and i tie them up tightly and then i double knot them. i stand up and stare through the broken window at the cloud. what am i to do now. in a shoe shop a woman is giving me a lolly. it's red. i am a polite and patient little boy i have broken the window and i enjoyed it. why am i not afraid of this thing. it came looking for me here it came hunting me why else would it be here. it came for me and it took account of me and then it left. i'm not afraid of it why am i not afraid of it. i suppose it could pounce and kill me instantly. no.

when i have tied my boots i go through the door out into the yard again i don't take anything with me there is nothing to take with me. i stand listening in the cloud it moves around me like it is alive this cloud i stretch out my arm and i can just see my hand i rise up into the air and i keep rising with my hands out-stretched either side of me up through the cloud up and up through the solid hill of cloud until i rise above it. all is blue up here all is so blue and the great yellow ball of fire in the sky is coming down on me and i look down onto this great rolling carpet of cloud and through it i see the yellow eyes of the cat and down i go i fly down through the cloud and i stand in front of the cat and it looks at me right into my eyes. yes. that is what i thought.

but how am i going to find the cat. where do i go how can i possibly know anything here. when i can just see my hand how could i possibly walk without stumbling without becoming lost forever if i walk out there surely i can never come back surely i will never find my way back to this place. but what do i have here anyway a broken window an empty matchbox a cold fire no food. the cloud is in the house now. i am going to walk and i am going to find it.

perhaps i have been standing here for an hour.

i can wait as long as i need to wait i can wait here the cloud moves around me as if it is exploring me sniffing me out becoming comfortable with my presence on these old stones. i feel like i have been standing on these old stones forever.

and there it is. i knew it would come there is the cry through the cloud there is the call on the moorland slopes. the sound of the cat high above me.

there it is again the long high keening of the creature. where is it coming from somewhere to the south i think. i wait perhaps another three minutes or four there it is again the long high call as soon as it begins i uproot myself from the stone and i walk towards it. i walk into the cloud until i am brought up against the drystone wall and i feel my way along to the right until i come to the wooden gate. i unlatch it and go through it i don't bother to close it behind me it is too late for that. i walk down the track as fast as i can i can see enough of the track in front of me to keep moving. i hear the noise again it is still ahead of me but it is very distant. i come down to the stream and i splash through it the water is icy on my ankles and my calves. i open my mouth i lie down in the stream and let it flow over me and let it flow through me until i am ice. i keep walking until the track turns left i know where i am the track here heads down to the valley but i'm not going that way i am sure the noise came from ahead of me from up on the tops. i strike out on a slight thin path through the heather if the cloud weren't down i could follow this path easily in the cloud i can only see heather a few yards in front of me all around me a circle of heather pink and purple flowers with tiny droplets of water on them. my wet trousers push through the heather. everything is silent now i think i am still heading towards the sound but the cat never stays still it never stays anywhere it is never where you expect it to be. it is ridiculous to follow the sound it is ridiculous to look for it i could walk this way for ever but it is too late now to stay at home.

in a building she stands before me and there is cloud between us. well she says i suppose you must do what you need to. i know what you think i say i know how it sounds i know god is dead i know he has been killed with everything else. i know all the parts have been taken out and are lying around on the carpet and now we are all free to be unhappy alone i know there is nothing holy now. perhaps i am circling it because it looks stupid to the people who take everything apart but i think there are things deep in some people which won't be taken apart i think that none of the things which make us move in the world can be pictured. the thin track through the heather is taking me upwards now up onto the slopes that lead to the shoulders of the moor. it must be ten minutes twenty maybe thirty since i heard it i think i am still heading in a straight line. the cloud takes away everything you think you know about where you are. well you do what you must do she says you go if you must but if you do not come back soon we will learn to live without you and you will lose her and me you will lose both of us forever. i hate her sometimes she sees through me she gives me no room at all christ her love fills me with shame. christ's trouble is that he's all human. where are the bears running through his bloodstream where is the sky and the water in him. he's all about the people you are god's chosen make the earth yours subdue it until it squeals what is underneath this what is beneath the waters. a man clad in gold stands in a wood and stares at me while strange birds wheel all around him. if you stare into the cloud long enough you can see shapes faces times a silent hunt riding above you fingers and claws the moving lips of lovers boats heading out to sea feathers and shells bees and blades vines and creepers growing from the sockets and the openings. it rises from the ground and sings to me and falls back under. i could walk this way forever.

i keep walking up my boots laced tight my feet and ankles cold and wet the heather rasping against my trousers at every step. i walk on and the silence and the stillness of this cloud and its closeness makes it all feel as if i am nowhere at all. i could walk this way forever i don't suppose anybody else would ever see me at all.

there is the sound again ahead of me and to my left and still far away i wonder if it is further now. i begin to walk faster one foot in front of the other up the tiny track through the heather and i keep walking and then suddenly the track ends and i step out onto a road. it is solid asphalt it stretches to my left and to my right off into the cloud there are no markings on the road and there is no traffic. i step out onto the centre of the road where now which way now. i decide to walk to the left i walk along the edge of the road and the sensation of the solidity the managed flatness under my feet is strange to me. i can't hear the cat. i wonder what to do i keep walking will i find the track to the house again now in this cloud how will i find it. then in front of me i see something rising in front of me on the other side of the road something is looming out of the cloud. i keep walking slowly towards it. it is a great rectangular shape as i move closer i can make out windows chimneys outbuildings.

it is a grey stone building it has an empty stretch of asphalt to its left with giant concrete cubes blocking the entranceway. there are grey metal shutters all over the windows with small round holes in them and the door is barred and padlocked i walk up to the door and rest my hand on the cold metal i make my way all around the building to the back following the walls with my hands in the cloud. there are some old sheds there and a barn with an arched doorway and a small garden with picnic tables. everything is weedy and overgrown. someone has forced the metal shutters off one of the ground floor windows here i'm able to push open the window and put my head inside. it smells of must and feathers shall i should i yes it is impossible not to accept this invitation.

i squeeze my way through the half open window into the inside of the building. i drop to the floor in a pile of pigeon shit there are spiders in the corners it is a tiny dank room i have landed in but there is a door to a bigger one. i walk through the door there are tables and chairs and a bar with handpumps there are old barrels lying in the corners it is dark but hundreds of pinpricks of light are coming in through the grey metal shutters on the windows they are like eyes the pinpricks of light are like yellow eyes looking at me from the outside. i should not be in here i can't look at the eyes i can't look at the shafts of light coming through they are like lasers they come through the windows and they land on me and each one burns me like acid. no this is terrible it should not be like this nobody told me about this. i need to find a place where the eyes of light will not land on me i run and crouch down behind the bar where it is dark there are plastic ashtrays scattered around on the floor and transparent pipes that come down from the pumps on the bar and disappear into the floorboards there is a brown plastic crate of empty beer bottles beside me. the light can't get me here the eyes cannot see me. but it is too much for me to be in here how will i get away from this place if i stand up the eyes will see me but then i wanted the eyes to see me that was what i wanted wasn't it it is so confusing in the cloud. i decide to make a break for it i hold my breath and then i scuttle on my hands and knees like a giant cockroach from the bar into the back room where the shafts of light from the metal shutters cannot come i almost trip over my own hands i think i feel one of them touching my skin on the way but it's fine. i am fine. i reach the small dank room and i run now to the window and i force myself back up and out through the crack into the curling cloud.

outside everything is clearer even in the cloud. that was a strange thing for me to do climbing into old buildings like that i am hunting here i am on a hunt what would i be doing in a building like that i was asking for it it serves me right really. i go into the garden and sit down on one of the picnic benches which creaks beneath me it is covered in beige and green lichens there is a rectangular green plastic ashtray in the middle of the table in which wet cigarette butts float in a pool of dark brown water i pick one up and sniff it i inhale the smell of the tobacco it is delicious. i wish i had a lighter here i wish i had some matches i would love a cigarette i am rolling a cigarette at a bus stop golden virginia i only buy small packs because i'm not really a smoker i take out a green paper and a pinch of tobacco and i pull the tobacco apart and spread it out evenly and then i begin to roll the paper between my fingers and thumbs i never use filters. i lick the edges delicately and glue the cigarette down i love this ritual i take a yellow plastic lighter from my coat pocket and i spark up and the first breath is always the best is really the only one worth having it lifts me up and i fly.

i see that there will be a time yes a time will come again not for lifetimes but it will come. the woods will be flooded as they were and hung with moss and we will take boats through them flat wooden boats and there will be no-one full enough to believe that any of the real things of the world could be counted or named. we will hear again the sound of the oars through the water and the sound that evil makes when it plays at being good and coming up from the ground we will be only what we were naked as in the old dance on the plains before we toppled the king and fell with him. down we fell down to where it first began but even here he can see us he can always see us there is no escape from him. hide in the mountain and he will find you hide in the forest and he will find you hide in the grave and he will find you. he will find you and pull you apart you will be torn into parts and those parts buried and a season will pass before a flower will grow from the soil you were sunk in. and that flower will become you born again complete but not the same and you will sit up on your bed in the tent on the fringe of the brown wood rubbing your crown three white hairs in your shock of black and a limp where there was none and you will ask of whoever is there or no-one at all you will ask lover what has happened to me?

there. the noise again. the cat again. there.

i think it is closer now perhaps it is coming from the same direction as before it is hard for me to tell now that the road and my expedition into this building have disorientated me but i stand up when i hear the noise and drop the cigarette butt and i turn around because it is coming from behind me. it is still there. yes it is closer it sounds throatier when it was circling me in the yard the noise was so loud i could hear its breath in my mind i could see its mouth open the pink wetness in there.

it is important that i pull myself together. this is not a game i have work to do. now i face the source of the sound and i begin again to walk towards it. i decide i will not walk around any obstacle in my way instead i will walk over it i will not be distracted i climb over three picnic tables and then reach the back wall of the garden which is stone. i climb up the stone wall and vault over it onto heather moorland. the call comes again it is straight ahead now you see this is the way to do things a straight line to the goal i keep walking i plough through the heather though there is no path i clamber over small rocks and some large ones i am heading uphill. the call comes again still straight ahead i laugh and i begin running slowly i bounce through the heather i keep bouncing like this until my right foot lands in a trench i didn't see and then i twist and fall heavily onto the ground. it's fine i'm not hurt i lie on the ground with my face pressed up against the heather there is the sound again but now it seems further away. just inches away from my head is a rock as big as my fist i was lucky. she is standing looking over the garden in the sun i come up behind her with the rock in my hand and i hit the back of her skull hard with it twice her head cracks and she falls to the ground then i take the child and hold it under the water until it stops kicking. i love you she says i love you too i say because you have to say that. then she puts her arms around me and we go back inside the house for dinner.

it was further away that time this is not good enough. i get up and i keep walking in the direction of the sound but i must have been walking for twenty minutes or so now and i have not heard it again. it seems to come in waves in clusters it rises and falls like the tides in the sea.

then i see something i'm sure i see something i'm sure i see a movement to my right it is so hard to tell the cloud is so thick i hold out my hand and still i can only just see my fingers but i'm sure something passed me it moved past me in the opposite direction to the one i am walking in. it went behind me.

i wonder if it would eat me. it must eat something up here where did it come from where would a creature like this come from you hear stories don't you nobody really knows anything. perhaps it would eat me perhaps that is what i am walking towards it feels as if that would be a fine ending. it springs from behind in the cloud i barely hear a thing i have no chance to move their jaws are so strong they go for the neck one bite one snap and that's it they are perfect creatures it would be a fine ending. all things become other things scales become tails feathers become hair legs become fins leaves become rocks why run from the change death brings. do i want the same thing forever my own cold soul clinging on in the cloud wrinkling drying up fearing the churning that wants me and will come. better to stand and wait as you should and welcome it. people are strange i don't understand them.

drop away drop away see how i run.

well i may not have seen anything. the cloud still seems to move around me as if it is alive as i walk i feel again how hungry i am if you get this hungry you begin to see things i'm sure i wish i had something to

eat perhaps there are bilberries here i have seen bilberries growing around the heather. yes. i drop to my
hands and knees and i start looking for berries i can't
see any i crawl steadily all around me in all directions i
don't know where i just keep looking now this is why i
was brought here you see there are bilberries here there
are dozens of the tiny little round blue berries hiding
under the heather. i pick them slowly and steadily with
my right hand until my left palm is full of them and
then i cram them into my mouth the taste is stunning
it is bitter and stunning and free. i keep crawling and
i keep picking perhaps six or eight handfuls of these
things there is nothing else in my life right now but
bilberries i could live forever on bilberries their beauty
is so strong.

after a while i begin to feel queasy. i have had enough
but perhaps this has saved me i feel stronger i feel i
could walk for days now i feel a new strength in me. it
left me it came to me and left me but it still wants me
because it's calling me it fed me when i was hungry i
have seen something that matters more than anybody
could know and i must find it. i sit with my hands in
my lap my hands stained purple the cloud embraces
me. in all of the crawling i have lost my sense of direction i don't know now which way to go still i know i

was heading up the hill so i will just keep heading up the hill and there will be something there for me.

when i was in the yard when the cat was circling me there was a smell it was a kind of waxy sharp smell and it moved with the sound and now i can smell it again. it is fainter but i smell it again here on the moor this is the smell of the cat it is as distinctive as the muscles around its shoulders there is such a power in this thing such silent power it is so pointed there is no waste about it. whatever it wants it gets this beast it is like a spear it goes right to the heart there is no turning away once you have seen this.

i stand up i orientate myself and i begin to walk up the heather hill again heather and cloud heather and cloud and my boots moving through them. suddenly i realise that my right boot has swung out into open air and my left boot follows before i can stop myself and now i am tumbling down into an emptiness that is eternal. i have come to the top of a cliff and i have fallen off or thrown myself off or thrown someone else off any of these would be fascinating. i turn over and around as i fall i had always thought that if i were to jump off a cliff i would be able to fly to control myself with my arms somehow to crash elegantly onto the rocks but no nothing works i flail and flap like i am boneless down and down and i will be eaten and if you have never been eaten then what are you. i remember i thought about this a lot but all of the thinking was meaningless none of it meant anything you can think for three decades and your thoughts will be worse than useless because you have not touched this thing not really. you have to live in this dimension your hands must be calloused your heart scarred or what are you.

honestly it is so difficult to concentrate out here the mind plays tricks in this cloud. i could have been here for days or years or minutes it all seems to just roll together i am floating across it all i am on a boat and now i see some distant coastline but there are no gapless lines of trees along the shore there are no clouds of birds bursting from the green and screeching into the sky there are no monkeys murmuring from bank to bank nothing flows that way now. someone found this place centuries ago and built a city here and now it's all neon and glass and contrails and rainbow slicks of diesel i am alone circling the world through oceans of plastic there is nothing left to find nothing to discover it's all gone i came too late.

now i think the ground is beginning to level out i must be coming up to the shoulder of the moor i don't know which part of the moor i am on i have no idea can i still detect the waxy smell somewhere in the cloud i think i can or perhaps i'm imagining it. maybe i am imagining all of it. maybe i can smell the cat but i can't hear it so how do i follow it how do i find it can cats see in cloud or are they like dogs do they need their sense of smell to find their prey. why did i use that word i will not be prey. if the cat wanted me for prey the cat could have had me so there must be something else happening here perhaps there is no cat at all if i told this story to somebody would they believe a word of it. somebody is sitting in front of me we are both sitting around a table and i am trying to explain what i have seen here. maybe they are a journalist or a doctor or some kind of cat investigator anyway they have a notebook i think this person is young maybe in their thirties and they have short brown hair and glasses. i think it is a man no it is a woman a man would scoff at me but a woman would listen she would have sympathy her hair is not short it is tied in a ponytail she is quite attractive she is beautiful actually. no this is a distraction this doesn't matter the point is that i am explaining to somebody i am explaining to this woman what i have seen here i saw a cat in the distance you see i saw it twice and then i went looking for it. can i prove it can i prove what can i prove it was here that i saw it do i have any photographs is there any evidence why would a cat be here. why would anybody listen to me has anybody ever listened to me i think she feels sorry for me she is making a big show of writing all this down but how do i know what she is writing i want to grab the notebook i want to rip it from her hands how do i know i can trust her how do i know what she thinks of me who is she going to give these notes to i haven't seen her identification. just because she is beautiful doesn't mean i can trust her.

i walk and walk it is flat now i have found some sort of thin track across what must be the shoulder of the moor another narrow peat pathway through the bowing heather. i would say it must be an hour or so maybe since i heard any sounds the cloud is not changing it is not getting thicker or thinner i am used to it now i have acclimatised it's fine but now something else is coming out of the cloud at me. ahead of me to my right a great tall shape and now another to my left there are two people walking towards me. they are heading right towards me walking straight at me one on my right and one on my left. now what are they doing here walking in this cloud walking straight at me through this cloud. they are coming for me they have found me. no they are not people no they are stones

standing stones i walk towards them until i am standing between them two great standing stones perhaps
eight feet high and behind them dimly at the edge of
the cloud two more. i walk from the first pair of stones
to the second when i reach the second i can see two
more just where the cloud thickens a stone row this is
a stone row. i put one foot gently in front of the other
and i walk up the avenue of stones i count the pairs as
i go six seven eight eleven twelve thirteen the stones
seem to shrink in size as the row goes on at the eight-
eenth pair they are shorter than me they are just about
up to my waist. after that the row stops.

i keep walking there is nothing else but heather
now the stone row just stopped it started and then it
stopped why did it not lead anywhere why would you
build something like that if it didn't lead anywhere. the
right thing to do would be to walk backwards at this
point. i start to walk backwards i put one foot behind
the other i do it very slowly because of the mist and
the heather. it is an intriguing thing to do this first you
feel your toes touch the ground then the balls of your
feet at the front and finally your heels everything is
the other way around you cannot see where you are
headed though in the cloud you cannot see where you
are headed when you walk forwards either so really

it is no different. i keep walking backwards and from behind me on either side the smallest pair of stones moves into view and begins to fade away in front of me into the cloud. eighteen times this happens the stones grow larger each time the sentinels appear from behind me and disappear before my eyes.

when i come to the last pair i keep walking i keep walking slowly backwards down the hill i come to a house and then a road i keep walking backwards i am in the lowlands now i walk through fields and through hedges and gateways there are people but they do not see me i am glad about that i keep walking over motorways and through towns and cities. i come to a town i walk down a street which seems familiar i continue to walk backwards down the pavement i look up at a window above a shop and i see two faces looking down on me a woman and a young girl. now what is that expression on their faces their hands are moving behind the glass. well i don't know anything about that. i keep walking i pass a school there is a playground full of children circling around and around something like wild dogs i hide in a corner until they have gone in i find myself lying on a bed with a girl she is a child i am a child we are wondering what to do next what happens if i touch you here well if you touch me i can touch you i suppose this is how it works that seems fair i think.

there seem to be birds scrabbling on the roof. i don't know what this woman is saying to me a minute ago she was shouting at me now she is putting her arms around me no it is not my fault we agree on that it's all fine really. if you keep walking backwards it emerges from behind you and then falls away again before you into the cloud and it is all fine really it is just like the wind blowing through and over you there is really no time to feel anything about it. i seem to be lying on the ground outside i don't think i wanted to be lying here the ground is hard beneath me. i keep walking.

i move out of the town past giant metal sheds and down dirty roads i pass through a wooden gate and now rushes and reeds grow up around me from behind. i walk backwards through the rushes and the reeds and on both sides of me black water spreads out and around i keep walking though i do not know what i am walking on. forests of rushes and reeds and great black trees come from behind me and fall away there are sounds on all sides now there is an island in the water and men on horses gather around it. i keep walking backwards into a forest there are pigs in the forest i can hear them grunting around there is a group of men one of them kneels on the floor now i am sure i have seen them before now what is this. a line of men on a hill falls back and down everything falls back and down you could keep walking this way forever everything grows green after a while and the sounds of the beasts are deeper and wilder. there is an ocean of stillness back here. i recommend walking backwards everybody should walk backwards at least some of the time.

but are there any cats here. no i have not seen any and it is a cat i am searching for i remember that the cat found me and left me and i must look into its yellow eyes because there are secrets there and i need to learn them. it is all very well looking backwards but what i am looking for is not here. i walk forwards instead over we go now through the cloud and heather for ever and ever it feels like forever that i have been here. maybe the stone row is an arrow that points to the cat i haven't heard the cat for a while i can't smell it now i don't think perhaps if i keep walking this way something will come. the ground begins to fall now to slope gently downwards the heather gives way to bracken here this is something new. and as i walk something else rises before me but it is not as tall as the stones and it is wider it is a low wall a low wall of earth. as i come up to it and look closer i can see that the earth is mounded and moulded around large stones which are embedded deep in the ground.

i turn right and i begin to follow this low wall which nearly comes up to my waist. after a while there is a gap in the wall i walk through the gap the cloud is still everywhere i come to a small circle of stones with some other stones scattered and buried in the ground inside it. i keep exploring there is more than one the low earth wall makes a circle around these smaller circles of stone it is like an old encampment or a village or something there i was right the stone row was pointing to something it was pointing here to this place. people lived up here that earth wall was a dyke with sharpened sticks around it there were sentries at the gate these little stone circles were houses there were fires in the grates in winter and thatch on the roofs look i am sitting on a flat stone in the middle of one of these circles it was a table or a fireplace or a bed a woman is sitting at the edge of the bed she has wild hair and hunched shoulders she is speaking in tongues she can see that up on the ridges walks a man with a staff and a wide hat she can see that a wolf plays around his feet and a raven around his shoulders she sees through the shadows cast on his face she looks into his one eye and she keeps speaking to him or to herself she keeps muttering.

outside is the sound of children playing it is not cloudy the sun is shining there is no heather or bracken there are wheat fields there are grapevines everything is abundant blue birds sing in the air the water is clean there are men with spears their faces are tattooed there are mangoes growing on trees outside there are apricots the skin of the people is weathered brown. there are goats in the pens inside the outer wall there are dogs barking there are cats the cats are here to keep the mice away from the wheat the cats are here to keep the place clean the cats are here to eat what must be eaten. if you have never been eaten then what are you.

i am hungry again i don't suppose there is anything to eat here there are no bilberries anyway i am sick of bilberries i never want to eat another berry. never mind hunger is just a feeling feelings come and go they are like worms inside you like birds passing over just watch them and they pass by. there is nothing to eat here and i cannot eat anyway until i have looked into its eyes it would bring me terrible bad luck to eat before i have looked into its eyes it would be an indulgence it would take me away. what i need is to empty myself. perhaps it has never looked into my eyes because i have failed because i am not empty.

now. there. hear that.

it is the cat again it is the scream of the cat it is coming from my left it is indistinct it is not close but i can hear it well enough i stand up i rise from the flat stone on which i was sitting and i turn to face the direction of the sound i stay precisely still until i hear it again. yes. it is some distance away but there it is calling me i begin to walk i cross two of the hut circles and when i come again to the embankment wall i shuffle myself over it and i keep walking through the bracken the bracken gives way to heather there are bilberries here but i will not stop there is no stopping now. i hear the cry again does it sound higher than it did before does it sound different i keep walking and the ground begins to slope downwards first gently and then steeply i lie down i put my arms by my side and i begin to roll down the slope i am rolling down the slope with my sister and we are both laughing. who can get to the bottom first she is older but i always win there is the smell of mown grass by the cricket pavilion in the park we get up together and we race to the water fountain she is older but i always win because i am faster. i drink for hours in the summer sun we will find our friends by the swings and dare each other to go right the way through the low tunnel where the stream goes under the railway line can you stand in the middle when the train passes over without running listen to that sound there is the sound again it is nearer. now there are rocks there are outcrops of granite and i am having to scramble down them there are ferns growing between the rocks now and there is the sound of water there is distant water running between the rocks there is the cry of the cat it is closer now. the sound of the cat and the sound of water singing under stones.

i reach the bottom of the rocks i hear the sound of water running but i cannot see water the cloud is still everywhere. i keep walking and i hit rocks again moving steeply upwards this is some sort of steep rocky valley with water there are tufts of grass and strange ferns growing from between the stones and always there is the sound of water. now again the sound of the cat it is close now it seems to echo as if it were coming from between the stones look at the stones i make my way down this rocky cleft and these great shapes loom from the mist and they are not shaped like the stones in the row they are sharp and wild and no human put them here. i hear the sound of water running where is the water coming from i squat down and listen i put my ear to the ground the water is under the ground there is a stream beneath me somewhere. i move slowly down the valley picking my way over the huge rocks. through the cloud great shapes come at me and fall away again there is the sound again there is the scream the cat is close. i keep heading down over the stones with the sound of the water i head towards the sound of the cat.

i almost put my foot down a deep hole in the rocks. i pull back just in time and grab an outcrop of granite to steady myself i hang onto the granite with both hands between my hands is a face something like a human but not quite human it stares out at me from the rock look at the grain of the granite in those eyes something is watching me here this is not a good place. i let go of the face i squat down and i peer down the dark hole the sound of water comes from deep below god this is a fearful place. what is down there what is beneath these rocks this is awful. something is rising what am i doing here i hear the scream again the scream of the cat but now it is behind me it is close behind me what is it doing this thing why is it screaming what is it. why would i be following some animal across a moor in this cloud how do i know what this is how do i know anything.

i stand up again quickly. the cloud moves around the rocks and the rocks seem to move in the cloud and now something touches my shoulder from behind i'm sure of it i'm sure something touched me a freezing wind blows across my body freezing water pours down my throat i turn around but i see nothing. i hear the scream again the scream of the cat now it is in front of me it is clear to me now how terrifying this is how stupid i have been to follow this thing how stupid i am to want to see it. this thing wishes me no good. here i am in a haunted gully with a river calling beneath me and a cat hunting me yes it is hunting me is it not clear is it not so clear how stupid i am. i am not hunting it it is hunting me and now it has found me.

the freezing wind rises in me the freezing water roars up to overcome me and i start to move as fast as i can but i cannot run among these rocks. i climb them but i must be careful if i twist my ankle if i fall and break something i will lie here and then i will be prey then i will be eaten i try to keep the wind from blowing me over i try to keep the freezing water from rising up my throat and drowning me i keep climbing i keep scrambling down the stone cleft. there is the cry again behind me it is no nearer and no further. it is following me it is playing with me it knows what it wants did i imagine it would look at me did i imagine i could charm it this thing is wild and it is hunting me. i don't stop moving i am so hungry the valley is steep the rocks plunge down but i keep going i keep moving over and around the granite hanging onto ferns and young trees growing between the teeth of the rocks i hear the scream again. the water runs under the rocks for ever and ever.

i come out after what seems like hours of this. the rocks grow further apart grass appears heather appears there is bracken and now there is a path there is an indistinct path leading down and now i can walk now i can run i run like i have never run before both my legs are so strong my body is a column of light and i will never go back. the scream comes from behind me again it is no further and no closer and i run i run away from the sound of the water and from the rocks and from the cat. the cloud is so close still i can see nothing i could run to my death at any minute but i will not stop running it is such a joy running like this all of your body comes together there is nothing but where you put your feet i am going to run for ever until i outrun this thing. come back she says don't run don't run from us you don't need to run you are too old to run there are things we can do which will mean you never have to run again we will help you. but i have to run because of all the things i see when i sit still and i cannot speak of any of it because i am so small.

i keep running into the cloud now i am running at the cloud and there is no time here nothing passes or begins or ends there is only the running and the cloud. the running is the cloud i am the cloud i curl around and outside myself i am everywhere i am the wind i slam into the rocks i break up and come together again i am a bird i am above the cloud now down through it now up again outstretched i am the body i am the mind i am the running and i am the breathing. at night in the garden or the forest or the field the sound of the earth turning over the soil breathing out on it goes breathing breathing it is the great animal and it makes you tiny it makes you nothing it dissolves you and makes you everything. through the cracks in the granite down under the gully it all opens out and look at the wonders under here i never knew of the wonders under here and all the time i was running across them running and running i am the sound i am the cat i am the rocks and the river under there we all move together where nothing begins and nothing ends. i am up now i am ahead of myself i turn back i see a man running through the cloud towards me i am brick i am stone he flows down from the heather onto a track he looks around him turns left keeps running with the wind with the cloud. he reaches a gate he falls across it he looks up with his eyes wide comes through the gate which is open runs through the door and closes it behind him.

home. i am home was this ever really home well it is now. there is a bolt on the inside of the door and i push it tight across i fall onto the seat at the table i breathe in great gulps as if my chest will break i look around for water but the can is empty. then i see the window god the window is broken there is no glass it could come in through the window why did i break the window what a fucking idiot i am i have got everything the wrong way round i am being hunted here there is no time for games. then i hear a cry i hear the sound it is right outside it is in the yard again. it has come jesus i have to block the window.

the table. there is nothing else big enough i move the mug off the tabletop and put it on the floor and i get to one end and start to lift the table up it is a great heavy old oak thing oh it is too heavy i can't lift it. i hear the sound in the yard again it is right outside surely it is right outside the cat it wants to eat me i have to lift the fucking table. i put everything i have into it i get the table up onto one end and i push it across the old wooden floorboards towards the window first one side and then another until the face of the table is pushed flat up against the wall and the legs stick out towards me. it is not high enough the top of the open window peeks out above the top of the table wisps of cloud come in through the gap the cat screams again.

what else do i have. i look around the room. the bed the bed is taller than the table i grab one of the lower legs of the table and begin to pull it away from the window. the cat screams again it is under the window. i run over to the bed i throw the sleeping bag onto the floor i pick up the mattress and lug it over to the window i shove the mattress up against the window and it covers it. i drag the table back to the wall trapping the mattress between the face of the table and the window the window is blocked but it is only blocked at the top by a mattress a mattress will not stop a big cat. well i have nothing better it is all i can do i run to the back door and make sure the bolt is secured all of the other windows are closed and locked. would a cat break through glass would a cat live on a moor i have had enough now enough of this.

i sit down on the chair again. the room is darker now that the window is covered with the mattress and the table some light comes in through the small window at the back and through the two small misted glass panels in the back door i don't want to look through the windows in case i see anything. i don't want to see anything i don't want to hear anything i don't want anything to touch me it is all ridiculous it will go away in time i don't want to hear anything if i hear anything i will drown in freezing water. but now there is no sound it has gone quiet my breath steadies i pick up the mug that was on the table there is a mouthful of water in it which i drink. it feels good to drink water it feels real i can feel my feet on the ground. i bend down and untie my boots and slip them off i take my socks off and press my warm sweaty feet down into the cold stone floor. it feels good this it feels real here i am again back where i was.

if any of it happened perhaps it will not happen anymore. i am just in this building in the mist on a moor and the mist will lift soon this kind of cloud can disorientate you the water has helped me to calm down i think i am very tired sleep will help. i look over at the bed and i see something under the bed frame that i couldn't see before i lifted the mattress off i know what it is but i don't want to believe it. i stand up and walk across to the bed and bend down and pick it up. it is a small purple wrapper a chocolate wrapper with half a chocolate bar inside. chocolate you see it is all normal again water and chocolate and my feet on the ground i am going to enjoy this. i go back to the chair and sit down and unwrap the chocolate slowly a deep brown smell comes up from the packet i drop the packet onto the floor and i finger the small squares on my lap. i take my time eating the chocolate i let it melt in my mouth it has nuts in it i am returned to everything that grows and is real. chocolate and water and my feet on the ground this is better.

there is a scream outside i run out into the garden someone is attacking my daughter. there is a man in a dark coat down there under the trees she is fighting back she is a strong one i run down there and i confront him. he turns to me i have seen his face before i punch him hard in the side of the head and he falls down but he gets up again quickly i kick him in the chest before he can rise and then i pick up a garden spade and smash it into his face. there is blood everywhere my daughter screams but i don't stop smacking him with the spade until he is down and he has stopped moving and then i don't stop either. his face is pulp it is not a face it is a crimson mash of blood and bone and hair i scream at it joyfully this is what a father is for you can do this they expect you to do this. i could cut this thing into pieces i could do it all again tomorrow i wish he would come every day. i pick up my daughter and she throws her arms around my shoulders and i carry her back into the house.

the scream comes from the back of the house this time. i will not look through the windows i do not want to see anything there is nothing i can do now i have done everything i can. there is a knife on top of the stove i pick up the knife and i run across the room to where my sleeping bag is strewn on the floor i pick it up with the pillow and i take them into a corner where i cannot see the back windows and i climb into my sleeping bag and pull it over my head. i zip it up as high as it will go and i take the knife down into the darkness of the bag with me i just wish it would stop screaming i cannot stand that noise not anymore that is not my noise not anymore. it is dark in here i am glad that i brought my knife i stretch my legs out into the depths of the sleeping bag and they do not touch the end i stretch them down further still they do not touch it i begin to shuffle down the bag but i do not find the end i keep shuffling in the darkness on and on i hold a knife in my hand a knife is always important everyone should have a knife with them because you never know what you will meet everybody used to carry knives now they won't let you the new dangers cannot be dispatched so easily i get down onto my hands and knees and i crawl down the tunnel into the darkness i keep crawling it is damp in here there is damp under my hands and my knees and there is damp in the air in the distance i hear the scream of a cat it is still out there it is still circling me it is circling the house circling the yard circling the moor round and round round and round you measure a circle beginning anywhere i keep crawling away from the noise i must get away from that noise from that thing it wants to eat me i keep crawling along the tunnel it is damp and now i feel things growing beneath my hands there is fur or moss or something beneath them on the floor of the tunnel the floor itself is soft it gives when i crawl it is warm here in the tunnel down i go along i go through the red darkness for hours and miles i go on my hands and knees the soft and warm and damp i cannot hear the cat now not anymore only this rushing now i see a light breaking over a green hill the tunnel opens out onto a yellow plain in front of me is a low stone wall i cross the wall i stand up and i begin walking towards the green hill i walk and walk and all around me swallows dive and speak and a gentle wind rolls over us in the middle of the plain is a great black tree it bends down towards me i bow my head to it as i pass i keep walking until i reach the hill and then i climb gently up the grass there is no heather no bracken no bilberries but anyway i am not hungry there is no hunger here i cannot think what hunger would be i walk up the hill i keep walking i realise i have no shoes or socks on the grass tickles me the swallows dive the wind rolls i reach the top of the hill there is a circle of low stones in the centre of its flat summit i walk across to the circle and enter it in the middle of the circle a woman sits she wears a red dress she is beautiful hello again i say i have been waiting a long time for you she says i am so thirsty would you fetch me water i have no water i say i don't know how i came here find me water she says no i am busy i say can't you see not this time she says not this time you are not busy fetch me water you may not cross the wall again until i have drunk i look back but there is no wall only the tree perhaps the tree has water i roll down the hill and walk back to the tree and begin to climb i climb right to the top i sit on the highest branch which bends beneath me but i do not fall water i say i keep saying the word water water water water water water i twine my arms around the branch and dangle my feet down i swing swing swing i stay like this for days if i look down perhaps i will see water the land grows dark there is darkness and now there is a sound the sound of a running stream in another three days the sun begins

- 156 -

to rise i cannot feel my arms i pull them i yank them hard they come free from the branch with a jerk and i fall crashing through the tree i hit branches on the way down i am bruised and cut i hit the ground i go through the ground i fall into a high bright cavern and all around me is water crashing over crystal rocks all of the colours of the world are here so this is what water is i have fallen into water i let it take me along and i listen to it speak drink drink drink drink the river takes me out onto the hilltop i collapse into the stones and here is the woman in the red dress she drinks and drinks and then smiles at me it wasn't so hard she says was it now you see what can be found i don't see i say i don't see anything and i want to go home but you have seen the water now she says i am scared i say of course you are she says of course you are you are such a young boy just look at what they did to you sometimes i feel like crying i say i am scared it comes in at me and jabs me i must be alert against it what might happen if it came in she says yes of course it is fine it is fine it is what you should feel it is alright to cry but i don't want to cry i say i want to kill somebody no she says you want to cry you are so young and they never told you look drink the water dissolves it and so i drink until i am quenched and then i kiss her no she says not this time there is the wall now go i touch her arm it is very hot in here i walk between two stones i step over the low wall i pick up my knife i drop my knife this is not that sort of world i listen but there is no sound i pull my head out of my sleeping bag and breathe the air of the room and i listen and there is no sound i don't think there has been a sound for weeks i sit up slowly i roll my sleeping bag down my body and step out of it there is a sound now but a low sound a gentle one i walk across to where the table and the mattress are pushed up against the window and i heave the table away and pull the mattress down onto the floor outside the window the pale cloud is thinner and now it is shifting and heaving in a low breeze that has arisen here i can see the wall of a building across the yard now it is gone again now it reappears the cloud is moving the wind is moving the cloud around i walk to the door and unbolt it and pull it open i step out onto the damp cobbles of the yard in my bare feet the breeze plays on my face the cloud dances around me my feet are warm on the cold stone there are gaps in the cloud now sudden and clean i see the gate and then the fence a broken roof a stone wall a scrap of tarpaulin an upturned tub a c

itting calmly, as if it were waiting for me, which I suppose it was, all this time. I won't pretend that everything is clear. Nothing is really clear, but this no longer seems to matter. I once thought that my challenge was to understand everything, to build a structure in my mind that would support all that I experienced in the world. But there is no structure that will not fall in the end and crush you under it.

The cloud is thinning by the minute. The cat is sitting on its haunches on the other side of the gate, facing down the track, away from me. It curls its tail slightly as it sits, and occasionally inclines its head to left or right. Its stillness always captivated me.

I don't want to follow it. I am very clear in my mind about that. I do not want to see it again, and I do not want to go any further with it. But now the cat rises and stands and begins to walk steadily down the track and I begin to walk after it. The cloud comes in and down, it thickens again and then empties itself. I see snatches of moorland as it drifts; the sides of hills, crests and slopes. I maintain a steady pace as I follow the cat. The animal walks off the track now and begins to incline up the slope of the moor. I keep following it. As I walk, something occurs to me: I can hear birdsong again. Somewhere up in the cloud hangs a single skylark, its notes rising and falling with the cloud and the wind. It keeps singing.

We keep walking, and the cloud parts on my left to reveal the wood with the pool at its centre. I can see where the cat is heading now. Soon the climb becomes steep and rocks begin to jut out from the sides of the hill. The higher we climb, the thinner the cloud gets. I pull myself up the granite outcrops, carefully and steadily, until I reach the uppermost rock of the tor, which lies flat like a tabletop on the granite stack at the highest point of the moor. The cloud is almost gone now, but drifts of it still blow around the outcrop of rocks. I look out in all directions at the great purple and green back of the moor rolling away towards the sea.

The cat is sitting again on its haunches a few feet away from me. It is even blacker than it appeared from a distance. It is huge. It doesn't seem especially interested in me. I wonder if I could touch it. After all this time, this thought is less of a strain to me. I walk gingerly over to the cat in my bare feet and slowly lay the palm of my right hand on its head, just between its ears. The flat of its head is wider than my hand. Its ears roll back slightly when I touch it. It is warm beneath my hands, but its coat feels rougher than I imagined it would. The cat turns its head back and regards me steadily. It has beautiful eyes. Beautiful, magnetic yellow eyes. Still, it is just a cat. I can hear the skylark again, below me now. I think the wind is getting up.

Acknowledgements

My editor at Faber & Faber, Lee Brackstone, believed in this book before I had written a word of it, which was a great privilege. After I had written the words, he pointed out all the unnecessary ones, and it is a much better book as a result.

My excellent agent Jessica Woollard has done so much over the last year to shape my writer's life into some kind of sustainable enterprise that I must owe her a good bottle of something.

My friends Jay Griffiths, Em Strang and Dougie Strang commented on this book in earlier drafts, and helped make it what it has become. Martin Shaw, friend and inspiration, has taught me much over the past five years about how the land tells stories and how to listen, and his work has influenced this book. Nina Lyon and George Monbiot pointed my research in revealing directions. My fellow editors and collectivees at the Dark Mountain Project, along with the many writers whose work I have read there over the past half decade, continue to inspire and provoke.

Finally, at the root of it all, my family are the soil

from which everything grows. I am steadily and happily grateful for my two brilliant children, my mum, and above all my wife, Jyoti, who welcomes the stories across the threshold, however disruptive they may sometimes be.